FLEEING THE SHADOWS

Dangerous Loyalties, Book Two

BOOKS BY PHYLLIS A. STILL

Dangerous Loyalties Series

Defiance on Indian Creek, Book One

Fleeing the Shadows, Book Two

Warrior on the Western Waters, Book Three

Palisades of the Heart, Book Four

To the descendants of the brave men, women, and children mentioned in this historical fictional account. Be strong!

Fleeing the Shadows

Dangerous Loyalties, Book Two

Phyllis A. Still

Climbing Tree Publications

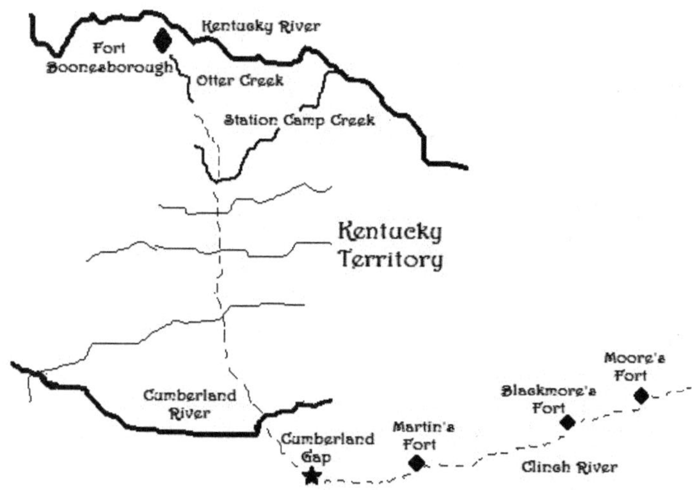
Kentucky River
Fort
Boonesborough
Otter Creek
Station Camp Creek
Kentucky
Territory
Cumberland
River
Cumberland
Gap
Martin's
Fort
Blackmore's
Fort
Moore's
Fort
Clinch River

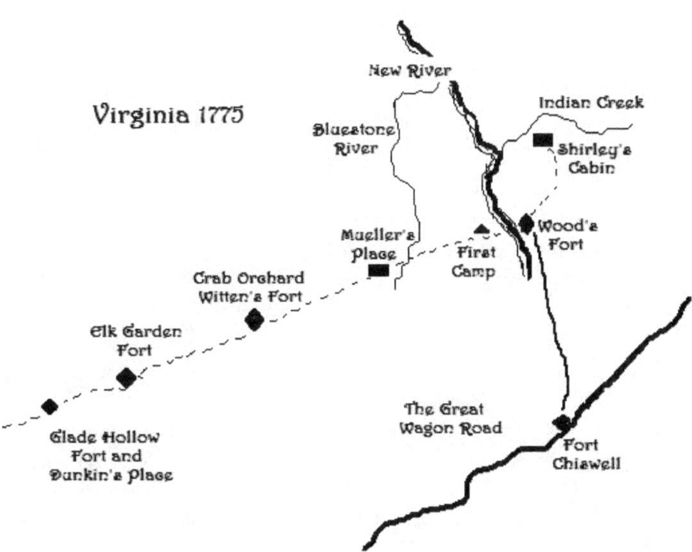

Virginia 1775
New River
Indian Creek
Bluestone
River
Shirley's
Cabin
Mueller's
Place
First
Camp
Wood's
Fort
Crab Orchard
Witten's Fort
Elk Garden
Fort
The Great
Wagon Road
Fort
Chiswell
Glade Hollow
Fort and
Dunkin's Place

Chapter One

August 23, 1775

My linen neckerchief flapped on the clothesline in the morning breeze. I took the garment in my hand and sighed. No matter how many times I'd scrubbed it with lye soap over the past week, the dirt stains remained. *But I can't make a rag of it yet.* I'd given it to a bartered slave named Adam, for saving my three-year-old brother Charlie from drowning. I swallowed a lump and blinked back tears. Adam and Big Jim fled from their owner that same day. I learned of Adam's capture ten days ago, from a vile Tory named Toloman, after seeing the neckerchief around his grungy neck.

My heart raced as the image of the evil Tories, Jinks, and Toloman flashed through my mind. They were the ones who had captured Adam and sold him to West Indies traders. They were also the ones who'd lured me with frying bacon the morning after delivering the dispatches.

And they were the ones who'd led me to the very Tories who were seeking Papa's life that night. It was Toloman who shoved me from my horse to the ground, injuring my shoulder.

I ignored the twinge of pain that remained there. *If I'd stayed hidden after delivering Papa's dispatches, we wouldn't be in danger. We could have left for Kentucky in time to catch the Boones. But I wouldn't have learned about Adam and recovered my neckerchief.*

I shook my head at the clothesline. *You're a fool, Mary Shirley. Why bother? It's ruined forever.* I adjusted the oval basket on my hip and stepped along the line, lifting the wooden clothespins from the neckerchief and Sally's diapers with my free hand. The fresh-scented wash fluttered into the basket.

It could have been worse. The Tories learned from Isaiah Brown that I wasn't a boy; he'd seen me before as a girl. Thanks to divine intervention, I got away from them, but Isaiah followed me. I shot him in the knee and escaped. *I hope he suffers for the rest of his life.* The last diaper landed in the pile.

I straightened my back, feeling proud. Papa said the documents were life-saving—something to do with a Tory named John Connolly allying the Shawnee to stay loyal to the king and raid the western settlements.

When I turned toward our two-story cabin, my stomach fluttered. Papa rode into the yard on Little Sis, and our dog, Drummer, stopped at the spring. I waved, but Papa's tense face gave me the shivers. He'd gone to Fort Culbertson before dawn. He wanted the latest news and to verify that the newlywed couple could still come tenant our farm in two days, when we removed to Kentucky.

I gripped the basket with both hands, sucking in the hot August air as he dismounted and rushed toward me.

"We have to leave as soon as we can load." He took the basket from my arms. "Cool Little Sis down for me while I carry this in and explain to Momma."

I grabbed the sleeve of his tan hunting shirt. "What's wrong?"

He clenched his jaw, and his slate-blue eyes searched mine. "My contact said Loyalists from Augusta County have offered a hundred-pound bounty on my head. If caught, I'll hang for treason against the king. We need to get to the safety of Wood's Fort by midafternoon. The McGuires have gone into hiding."

I stepped back, fighting tears. *Why did I have to brag to Toloman about acquiring my fast horse from William McGuire?*

Papa lay his free hand on my arm. "It's not your fault. They would have been after me for divulging their plan sooner or later, anyway. God is watching out for us. Once we get some miles behind us, we'll be able to catch our breath again." He rushed into the cabin.

It is my fault, and now the McGuires are in danger too. I blinked away tears and rotated the stiffness from my shoulder. *No time to cry.* My heart pounded as I removed the mare's saddle and hoisted it over the fence rail. I walked her around the yard once, then led her out to graze. *At least my foot's mostly healed.* A ruptured blister had festered, and Momma had scraped the infection out.

The cabin door flung open so fast the metal hinges didn't have time to squeak. My eight-year-old brother, George, leapt from the porch and sprinted to the barn. "We're going. We're finally going."

Drummer pranced to my feet and rolled to his back. I knelt and rubbed his creamy belly. "Good boy. Rest now. We're leaving soon." I stood, glancing beyond the wilted oak leaves into the depth of blue above, and whispered, "Lord, help us," before rushing into the cabin.

Momma seemed to be flying from one dark corner to the next, gathering items into bundles, and setting them on the rectangular table. "Land sakes, I thought I had this thought out, but my mind is like porridge. And I wanted to leave the cabin scrubbed clean, but Mrs. McCarley will just have to forgive us."

Papa touched her shoulder, and she stood still. "Take a deep breath, *liebchen*. You've packed well, and the McCarley's are excited about moving in today." He kissed her cheek. "Make piles on the porch. I'm going to the barn to help George saddle the horses."

I pulled my neckerchief from the basket with a sigh and climbed the ladder to the loft.

White hazy light streamed in from the open shutters. A lump formed in my throat at the sight of my younger sisters, Katie and Lizzy. I glanced around, regretting every fuss I'd had with them and George in our loft. For the next few weeks, we'd be sharing a small canvas tent on the ground. *Then we'll really have something to complain about.*

They were rolling their blankets with the blue-striped ticking still full of straw.

I shook my head. "You'll have to dump the straw from the ticking before Papa can pack your bedroll behind the saddle rim."

"Oh. I forgot." Twelve-year-old Katie shoved the bundle back out flat. "Wish we could keep it. I'm not looking forward to sleeping on the hard ground."

Nine-year-old Lizzy sighed and gave hers a kick to unroll. "Maybe there'll be enough leaves to gather under us each night."

I knelt before my pallet. "Maybe there'll be some comfortable places to sleep in the forts we pass through, but most likely not. It's best to expect the most miserable conditions you can imagine. But you'll get used to it once you're exhausted enough. I did. The rocks won't even bother you."

Lizzy frowned at me a moment, then removed her blankets.

I pulled my gray woolen blankets from my bedding and yelled, "Look out below" before dropping them. After rolling my ticking, I stepped to my hope box and spread my neckerchief on the floor. I placed my keepsakes on top, then gathered the cloth around them and tied it into a bundle with a sigh. *All my dreams packed away for the future.* The treasures were placed into my knapsack on top of my extra outfit, stockings, and undergarments. I draped the bag over my shoulder, tucked my bed under my arm, and descended the ladder, dodging my youngest sisters. Susie, Nancy, and seventeen-month-old Sally were attempting to fold the pile of blankets.

I hurried to the side of the barn and unfurled the ticking, untied the end, and emptied the straw into a pile of old hay.

Katie stepped beside me, shaking out her tick. I sneezed.

"Oh, sorry. I should have waited until you moved." She snickered and glanced at me.

In response to my just-you-wait glare, she grinned and flipped her braid at me with her hand, then sprinted to the barn laughing. She had become almost like a friend these past five days, losing whatever animosity she had for me.

If she could trade places with me for a month, she'd know how hard it is not to be bossy. I chuckled and took my time strolling back inside to help Momma collect the last of the items we could take while everyone else helped Papa.

All our furniture and household items would belong to the new couple, even if we didn't stay in Kentucky, including Katie's bearskin rug. She and George had been checking traps when the black bear lunged at them. She shot it in the chest, and Papa said she'd earned the right to keep it. Now, only items needed to survive the trip could be loaded on the horses and on Gideon, our mule.

Momma handed me one of the loaves of sourdough bread she had baked early this morning, then covered a second loaf on the table beside a knife and the rest of the butter. "It will make a nice welcome gift for the McCarleys." She glanced around and released a deep sigh. "We've only lived here a year and a half, and now we start over again—with nothing. I hope this move will be our last. Land sakes. Listen to me grumble."

I stepped to her side, placing my arm around her waist, and rested my head on her shoulder. "I hope so too. How am I ever supposed to meet someone to marry someday if we never have a permanent home?"

Momma laughed. "Well. The sooner we get there, the sooner we can get settled." She turned and pulled me into a cozy hug.

I didn't want to move. She stepped back first and wiped her check. "Lord, be with us."

I squeezed my eyes closed to keep them from watering and shut the creaking door for the last time.

When I turned toward the yard, my jaw dropped. Each horse was draped with bags and pouches, in addition to overstuffed saddlebags. But poor Gideon. If we placed one more item on him, he'd topple.

"Well, now." Papa stood back, scratching his head. "If we've forgotten anything, it must not be important. Gather around so you can hear." He waited until we circled him. "We'll ride the horses today because we need to rush to Wood's Fort and get across New River before making camp. But the horses aren't used to carrying so much weight. After today, expect to walk most of the way to Kentucky."

"How long will it take?" I dreaded to hear.

"Less than a month, I hope. Now, we'll pray." Papa bowed his head. "We ask for a safe, swift journey to Fort Boonesborough. Give us strength, wisdom, and peace. Bless the McCarleys while they abide in this home with the same abundance you provided for us. Amen."

"Go Tucky?" Charlie asked.

"Yes, we are going to Ken-tucky." Momma enunciated.

My stomach churned with the reality of leaving. A fast scan of my brothers revealed grins. My sisters were wide-eyed and solemn. My heart was racing.

I glanced at the sun shimmering through the trees at the midmorning position and wiped sweat from my temples. *It's already miserable.*

Papa made one more inspection of the horses, then helped my sisters mount in pairs, Katie with five-year-old Nancy and Lizzy with Susie, who was not quite seven.

George heaved himself into the saddle on his yellow dun and tipped his new hat at me, grinning. It had a wider brim than the one I had borrowed but had to leave behind when I fled my Tory captors.

I chuckled. "It makes you look too grown-up."

He jutted his chin, still smiling, and moved toward Papa.

Momma mounted with a pleasant smile that gave the appearance of peace, but her eyes were narrow and serious. During the last ten months, I'd witnessed Momma maintain a strong facade while dealing with Papa's long absences on survey jobs. Even pregnant, with whoever would be my eighth sibling by February, she appeared strong and resolute. Papa placed seventeen-month-old Sally in front of her. The toddler rocked forward. "Giddy up."

Momma clasped the child's belly. "Be still. You'll spook him." Then she turned to me. "Are you able to manage Charlie, or shall I have Katie take him?"

"I can hold him." I smiled and mounted my sleek red sorrel. "I'll give him to Katie if my arm weakens." Katie lacked the patience needed for the rambunctious boy. Being fussed at made him more belligerent. *I must be strong. Momma needs me.*

Papa lifted Charlie into place in front of me. He whined and squirmed. "Need to pee."

I shook my head. "Why didn't you tell Papa before you got up here?" I slid off and caught Charlie in my left arm as he lunged. "Does anybody else need to go to the privy?" *It's going to be a long trip.*

"Me." Nancy followed.

Susie rushed to my side. "I'd better go again too."

Papa shook his head, laughing. "Well, so much for being in a hurry."

After situating Charlie in the saddle again, he kicked Rebel's neck and shouted, "Get up." The horse stretched his head toward the offending child's leg with chomping teeth.

I clasped Charlie's leg. "Be still now. Horses don't like being kicked in the neck, and Rebel almost bit you."

He sat still.

Katie led her rust-colored horse up beside me. "Need me to take Charlie?"

"No, but I'll holler if I change my mind. Thank you."

Katie shrugged. "Well, yell if you need us to come back." She trotted into position behind George.

Papa cantered past us all. "Stay in single file, like we've been practicing."

He led the way, and Momma's horse, Sir, moved forward, followed by Lizzy and Susie on the sweet dapple-gray I had named Patriot. Drummer raced ahead of Papa to sniff out a rabbit hiding between boulders. George sat tall and kept General's gait smooth. Katie glanced beyond me at the cabin and sighed before easing Rusty along.

I didn't look back as the safe, comfortable cabin shrank behind us. The horses loped down the southeastern trail past the garden and the tobacco fields. Tears rolled down my cheeks as Big Jim and Adam came to mind again. Papa had borrowed the slaves to help build tobacco mounds, and we had grown fond of them. I had to glance back, picturing them in the field working and waving with big smiles. *Goodbye.* I blinked away tears and urged Rebel into a trot to catch up.

At the two-mile mark, where Indian Creek veered northerly, Rebel nickered and bobbed his head. My throat constricted and my heart fluttered. "Easy, boy. We aren't going that way again." It was the route we'd taken to make the delivery.

Papa halted us a few yards further. "Hop down for a quick check of the horses. It'll be another hour before we stop again."

Still jittery, I checked Rebel's hooves and legs, then took time to rub his neck. "Good boy." Talking to him calmed me, and he nickered with the attention. "I know. We're still scared. But at least we aren't alone this time." I checked his saddle and mounted.

Moments later, we headed south along the western edge of Fitz Run. A sudden pain gripped my chest and sped my heart. *Jinks and Toloman were on their way to Wood's Fort. What if they escaped the waylay? What if they're at the fort?* Wood's Fort was near the Great Wagon Road that leads north to Pennsylvania and south through Virginia and beyond. *How many Tory spies are there watching for us?* Bile rose into my throat. I swallowed and sucked in deep breaths.

As my family sauntered up the shaded trail, I urged Rebel into a slow trot and focused on Charlie's repetitive little song about going to Kentucky. Flickers of sunlight danced through the treetops and onto the trail of decaying leaves and pine straw—*like...eerie...little...fairies.* The shadowy images made me shiver. I closed my eyes and sucked in a deep breath. *Stop imagining.* I moved Rebel into a canter.

We loped along at a rushed pace for an hour before Papa held up his hand and stopped.

"We'll rest the horses a few minutes and eat a bite of lunch—but stay close." His voice sounded tense. He glanced around the perimeter before dismounting.

My head throbbed. *Worry is making me ill.* I blew out a breath and lowered Charlie to the ground by one arm and slid off, tapping his shoulder. "You're the goose." I ran, and he grinned, then raced to Nancy, repeating the game. The chase was on until Momma called us to come eat.

Too soon, Papa called, "Time to go. We have another two hours before we reach the fort." We mounted out of breath, but Charlie and my stomach had stopped fidgeting.

"Once we leave Wood's Fort, our games must be quiet," Papa said.

Momma smirked at him. "But for today, the children's laughter is a good remedy for my worries."

Papa smiled and tipped his hat at her, then led us in a fast pace along the leaf-mulched trail through ancient trees full of woodland creatures fleeing before us.

Are Momma's worries the same as mine? Are we outrunning the storm behind us only to rush into a whirlwind? I shook my head. *Stop that! Once we're at Fort Boonesborough, life will settle down.*

I smiled and began picturing a thriving community preparing for a harvest dance in October.

Chapter Two

The clanking of a blacksmith's hammer alternated with the thud of axes chopping wood as we neared Wood's Fort. When we rounded a bend in the trail, a blockhouse jutted over the tall log pickets. Uproarious laughter inside the enclosure, mixed with occasional swearing, knotted my stomach. *God protect Papa.*

Most of the men, coming and going through the double-doored gate, wore common linen hunting shirts, but a few donned various shades of a blue-wool uniform. Some of the jackets were trimmed with red bands, others with gold. These men wore their hat brims flipped up on one side with a brass rosette—*the same as Jinks's.* My breaths shallowed as I scanned the faces of the men. None looked familiar, nor hobbled on one leg as Isaiah would.

Smoke from several fire pits wafted toward me and made me cough. I dismounted beside my family in the shade of an old oak.

"Wait here and don't wander off." Papa made hurried steps toward the opposite corner's blockhouse.

He didn't have to worry about me. I eased closer to Momma, where my wide-eyed younger siblings stood holding hands. George smiled and returned chin-raising greetings from the men who passed by.

Katie turned toward me. "Why don't we just stay at this fort? Seems to be plenty of men to keep us safe." She smiled at a young man gawking at her with a grin.

Shocked, I pulled her sleeve and glared into her eyes, whispering, "Look away. He shouldn't be ogling you like that."

"Pshaw." She wiggled her head. "No harm in being friendly."

"We can't risk being friendly." I took a deep breath. "They might be Tories on the lookout for Papa. Mind what I say, or I'll tell Momma."

She huffed and moved away from me.

As Papa returned with more gunpowder and a slab of salted pork, his eyes were narrow, and his jaw clenched.

Bad news?

He attached the bags to Gideon, removed a portion of rope, and turned toward us, motioning to come. He squatted and patted his leg. Drummer scampered beside him, sitting with his tail sweeping the dirt. Papa ruffled his fur, then attached a rope to the leather collar.

I held my breath. *What is he doing? He's never put a rope on Drummer before.*

"We must be as quiet as possible from here on out." His lips pressed together.

Surely, we aren't leaving him! A lump swelled in my throat as my eyes watered.

Papa stood, glancing at each of us. "That means Drummer has to be a watchdog now and stay tied up. No more playing for him."

A relieved sigh escaped, but I felt sorry for Drummer.

"He must stay with me while I train him to obey silent commands. Understand? You may snuggle him one more time, then not again until I say. I've neglected this part of his training."

My heart fluttered and my neck pulsed. *He's heard something troubling.*

As everyone stepped back toward the horses, I followed Papa, whispering, "What is the news?"

He glanced at me, then up at the tree limbs before brushing a loose strand of long black hair back under his round-brimmed hat. "Sure you want to know?"

"Yes, sir." My throat felt dry. "I'm not good at pretending everything is all right." I swallowed. "My imagination makes things worse."

He leaned toward me. His breath tickled my ear. "The dispatch you delivered made it to the intended parties and is on its way to contacts east and west. But the Augusta

County men are half a day away from our cabin. They've hired Indians to watch for us and report our positions. Want me to continue?" He raised his eyebrows.

Blood rushed to my feet, but I nodded.

"Once across the river, we'll head up the old hunter's trail to the ridgeline that connects the forts being built near the Clinch River. It's a harder way to take the children, but faster and safer for us. My scout friends are spreading misinformation that we're taking the Wagon Road south to Fort Chiswell and joining others traveling the Boone trail." He stepped back, wiping sweat from his brow. "Ready to get started?" He grinned and started toward the horses.

No. But my head nodded. "Was there news of the McGuires?"

He hesitated, but continued his course.

I mounted Rebel with a heavy heart and a secret longing that they would come to Fort Boonesborough and hide out with us. I glimpsed a couple of men watching us from a few feet away and glared at them. They tipped their hats and resumed activity. I focused on the back of Papa's head as he led us through the gate.

Papa kept to a fast pace, which made me have to squeeze Rebel tighter with my thighs and straighten Charlie each time he slid sideways.

After an hour, the trail turned marshy and muddy smelling. Mosquitoes buzzed around my ears, and soon my neck and cheeks itched. Charlie scratched his neck and whined. "'Squitoes."

"Try not to scratch. You'll only make the itch worse. Momma has a remedy for us to use as soon as we stop. Be still."

Papa led us out of the bog and onto a grassy meadow near a small creek. "The New River crossing is another hour and a half. We're making good time. Once across, we'll make camp."

We dismounted, and the horses whinnied on their way to a plot of grass in the shade. Charlie ran into a thicket to relieve himself, and George followed.

Momma rubbed her cheek. "There was such a hurry this morning, we forgot to apply mosquito ointment." She opened the pouch of pungent turpentine and bear grease. "Come to me when you finish in the bushes."

"Ew." Sally coughed and wrinkled her nose as Momma slathered her with the salve, then treated herself.

Along with soothing the itch, the vapors invigorated my breathing, but my nose and eyes watered. I hoisted Charlie onto Rebel and looked back down the trail from which we came. By now, the new couple would be settled into our cabin on Indian Creek. I sighed. *Most likely we'll never be back.* I placed my foot in the stirrup, then wiggled onto the saddle behind Charlie. The family trotted ahead. My rear was so numb from having to sit farther back on the saddle that I longed to walk.

At our last stop, Papa took a few minutes to check the surrounding area. His face seemed relaxed. "We are far enough away that you can ride close and talk if you want. Might help relieve the boredom and saddle-soreness."

I sighed, rubbed an itchy place behind my knee, and slowed Rebel to keep my distance from Lizzy and Susie. The two never seemed at a loss for something to prattle on about. I preferred the calming sounds of the Allegheny woodlands behind us, but Charlie hummed an off-tuned version of the frog-courting song that made my head pound before it ended.

I covered his mouth with my hand. "Listen."

He pulled my hand away and glanced around.

"Can you hear the sweet chirps of robins, cardinals, and sparrows?"

His head cocked to the side a moment, then he shrugged. "Sing frog."

I sighed. "All right but let me lead. You have it all wrong. And don't sing loud—you'll send the crows fleeing."

I sang with Charlie and chuckled as we passed a family of chattering squirrels in the trees overhead. "I don't think they like our singing."

A new itch a little further up my thigh made me gasp. *Chiggers!* I squeezed Charlie's belly and urged Rebel into a gallop to catch up with Momma. "I have chiggers."

She nodded. "I've been feeling itches myself, but we'll have to wait until we get to the river to find relief. They must have found us at our first stop in the meadow. Thankfully, we'll make camp once we cross."

"Yes, ma'am." I fell back, dreading the misery another hour would bring to unmentionable places under my petticoat.

Papa had Drummer's rope tied harness-style by the time we all gathered at the bank. "This crossing will be a good test. It's swift, but not too deep for the horses. I'll take Sally and Momma across first, then come back and forth for each of you. Don't be afraid."

He reached for Sally, secured her with his left arm, and descended the bank, with Momma following. I held my breath, and my heart raced. Slow and steady, the horses waded into the shimmering green water, and Drummer swam beside Papa's horse. Momma's petticoat filled with air and floated as her legs submerged with Sir. The horse swam a few feet before stumbling to stand. I exhaled and scratched my knee. *They made it.* Momma scratched at her lower leg, then took Sally from Papa as Drummer shook water on them.

"Come ahead, Mary," Papa shouted and waved. He rode Little Sis into the river, but stopped short of the deep point. "Hold the reins tight and ease Rebel down slow. You can do this. I'm here if you need me."

He wants me to do this...alone? I sucked in a breath, blew it out hard, and held Charlie tight as Rebel obeyed my tongue-click. The horse headed down the bank without hesitating. My stomach knotted as the water reached my thighs. *At least the itching has stopped.* Charlie whimpered. I snuggled him tighter, hoping he'd relax. "It's all right. If you end up in the river, roll to your back and float. Papa will get you." My stomach knotted at the thought. He leaned forward, squeezing the saddle.

Rebel stepped sure-footed along the riverbed and up the bank before I released a deep sigh of relief.

"Yippee!" Charlie shouted and clapped.

My arms trembled with fatigue as I passed Papa.

"Good job. I knew you could do it." He grinned.

After easing Charlie to the ground, I dismounted onto shaky legs, then hugged Rebel's neck. "Good boy. Thank you."

"I can't watch anymore." Momma turned away. "Please tell me he's not going to let the rest of my children cross alone." She stepped toward her horse.

"He's gone across, but he's letting Katie keep Nancy." I glanced at Momma and scratched my leg.

She shook her head. "Land sakes. I'm going to get the lye soap ready for scrubbing off these vile chiggers. Don't tell me anything more unless someone falls in."

"Yes, ma'am." I smiled and gazed back to the river crossing while rubbing a new itch on my waist. *I hope we have enough ointment.*

Katie emerged safely from the water, grinning. "That was fun."

"No." Nancy shook her head with wide eyes. "It was scary. You didn't hold me tight enough, and I started floating off the saddle."

Katie wiggled her head and scratched her upper thigh. "Well, you know how to swim, silly."

I ignored the rest of their banter and watched Papa hoist Susie onto his saddle.

Lizzy made the crossing without a problem. I waited until Papa deposited Susie on the ground, then went to him. "Momma won't like it if you let George come alone."

He glanced at me, then at Momma, and smiled. "Duly noted. George is strong enough and confident. I'll get forgiveness later." He grinned before riding back to the deep water and waved George forward.

My heart raced. I glanced back at Momma, who looked down with a loud huff and chopped a bar of soap into chunks on a stump.

Papa's in trouble. I smirked and looked toward George. Papa was leading General by rope toward the bank. My heart did a flip. *What did I miss? Did Momma see?*

Momma rushed to the bank with her hands on her hips.

Papa stepped from his horse with a sheepish grin. "General was a bit skittish. But with a little more practice, George will learn how to calm him." He looked past Momma's glare. "I'm proud of all of you. We'll make camp and set out tomorrow when we're rested." He rubbed his thigh as he smiled again at Momma. "Now, let's get these blasted chiggers washed off. If I were alone, I'd go into the woods for a good scratching session with some rough bark, then bathe in the coldest mountain stream I could find, followed by a good dousing of corn liquor. That's the soldiers' cure for chiggers."

He laughed, but Momma didn't. Her eyes remained narrowed; her chest rose, then fell. With a shake of her head, she stormed up the bank away from Papa. She drew a deep breath when she came to a stop. "Swim under the water to be thoroughly doused, then come to me, and I'll rub your clothes down with lye soap on the outside. You'll each take a sliver of soap back into the river to wash your bodies and rinse. Don't forget your private parts."

I scratched my ankle and glanced at Papa, who seemed to be taking his time walking Little Sis into camp. He slunk toward George. "We'll unload and tend to the horses so you girls can go first."

"We'll need a privacy blanket strung up first." Momma's tone was curt as she rubbed her belly.

Plunging into the cold water made me shiver and calmed my irritation at Papa's callousness. *He knows*

Momma is worried. I went under the water for better modesty and vigorously scrubbed the itchy welts scattered from my ankles to my privates. I even had some bites under my left arm.

After air-drying, I took my turn behind the privacy blanket, rubbing turpentine grease all over to repel the insects but also to relieve the itch.

"It's been an exhausting day." Momma's face drooped as she unloaded a few utensils for meal preparation. The younger girls played chase and conquer the log with Charlie while Papa and George took their turns in the river.

When they emerged, Papa motioned for me, Katie, and Lizzy to come. He pointed to a flat area between two large oaks. "I'll tie a rope between these trees for the larger tent." He glanced toward a semi-cleared spot on the opposite side of camp. "The smaller tent will go there. Bring the canvases to each location before unfurling and don't lose the iron spikes rolled inside."

"Yes, sir," echoed as we went to the pile of supplies. The larger tent was heavy, but George and I managed it while Katie and Lizzy carried the smaller one. At the trees, Papa, George, and I hoisted the canvases over the ropes in a lean-to style—taller in the front than in the back. Katie and Lizzy stretched the ends out as far as they could while Papa drove the spikes through to stake the canvas down. The exposed triangular ends each had a cloth draped over so we could lower them to help keep out unwanted animals. The fact that anything could get in anyway was unsettling.

With the last stake driven, Papa stepped back, nodding. "The tent is ready for bedding. George and I will bring back small game for supper and set out some traps."

Katie, Lizzy, and I made beds for Momma, Papa, and the four youngest children in the larger tent, but the smaller tent didn't look big enough for four. I stepped back, shaking my head. "We can put our bedrolls inside and decide who sleeps where later."

"Suits me." Katie tossed her pallet toward the back.

Lizzy unrolled her bed along the left side. "I want here. Now, let's go gather blackberries."

The two raced ahead of me to a thicket, then poked through the vines with sticks but not taking the time to examine the area before plucking berries. My stomach did a flip. *Land sakes.* "Watch for snakes."

Lizzy glanced at me and resumed picking.

"Don't you think we know that by now, Miss Bossy?" Katie's tone was sarcastic, but she wiggled her head, grinning. "We aren't infants." She held out a handful of berries. "Want some?"

I smiled and took half, but a pang of hurt lingered. "Thank you. I'm sorry. It's just my nature to worry, I suppose."

Katie glanced into the treetops and sighed. "Well, maybe you should pray more and leave the worries to God and Papa. I'm excited about the trip. Momma said Fort Boonesborough will become a township as soon as enough settlers arrive, and I'm looking forward to making friends with girls my age. Won't it be grand?"

Not sure if she meant to sound mean, I remained calm. "Yes, but I hope we don't grow apart. I like us being friends."

She lay her free hand on my shoulder. "You'll always be my first friend because you're my sister and only sixteen months older. But I want friends my age who don't worry so much and aren't bossy." She flashed purple teeth at me and waited for my reaction.

I raised my chin and grinned. "I understand. But as the eldest, I reserve the right to boss you." We took turns smiling at each other with blackberry-stained teeth and giggling.

"If you girls are finished with the tents, I need help gathering greens. And we need fresh water." Momma held out two baskets and the wooden canteens.

"I'll go for water." I draped the clunky canteens on my shoulder and strolled to the river, thankful for the sweet bond developing between Katie and me. *She finally seems to respect me.*

Chapter Three

Sweat trickled down my thighs as I neared the bank. I lifted and ruffled my petticoat before plopping down on a cool, grassy slope. After removing my moccasins, I plunged my feet into the cold rippling current and lay on my back. Wispy gold-rimmed clouds sailed across a sky of fading blues and deepening shades of amber.

"Mary," Katie yelled. "What are you doing napping while the rest of us work?"

My eyes popped open. *Why is she so harsh?* "I didn't mean to doze off." I stood, shaking off dirt. "Why are you being so cross?"

She frowned and stormed off in the direction of a patch of egg-shaped plantain leaves nearby.

Lizzy handed me a basket and paring knife. "Take over for me. Momma needs the water." She took the canteens and dipped them in the river.

I knelt before a small patch of white dandelion heads, plucked one, and blew. The tiny seeds fell straight down instead of blowing away in the wind. *Can't even make a wish for a safe trip to Kentucky.* I shook my head. *Shouldn't be believing in fairy tales, anyway.*

I snipped the leaves off with one hand, dropped them into the basket, and then went toward the plantain where Katie was supposed to be. "Where are you? You aren't supposed to go off without telling someone."

She didn't answer.

An acorn hit me on the back of the head, followed by another. "Stop that." I turned to fuss at Katie, but a man stood stoic and still in front of me.

My arms flew into the air. I lost the basket and almost the content of my bladder before the scream came out. Tiny leaves flitted to the ground around me as Papa pulled me into his arms. "It's me. Breathe."

My heart raced as I took another breath and swallowed hard to avoid throwing up. Flashbacks of the night I delivered Papa's dispatches made my knees buckle.

Papa kept me from falling. "You girls weren't listening, nor watching for bent twigs and moccasin prints." Papa's serious face matched his tone.

My insides trembled.

Katie emerged from the shrubs, frowning. George leapt out, holding up long sticks with several impaled squirrels.

"We were able to sneak up on you." He laughed. "Papa snatched Katie before she could whimper."

"We're fair game for roaming Cherokee and Shawnee hunting parties. Scouts, from Wood's Fort, confirmed that the Cherokee are scouting for the Tories. You have to stay alert, even this close to camp."

"I thought we were still in a safe area." Katie sniffled and wiped a tear from her eye.

I ran to the shrubs, heaved, and then wiped my mouth on a corner of my apron. *How could Papa scare me so?*

George and Katie headed back to camp, but Papa waited for me.

"I'm sorry to add to your fears. But being captured by Indians would be far worse than anything you've already experienced."

I fell onto his chest, weeping.

He stroked the back of my head. "I'm sorry, polliwog. I hope our lives won't always be so hard. We have to keep going—even when afraid. Remain strong and hold on to hope."

I sniffled and stepped away, retrieving my now cracked basket that lay near a large rock. "I have to collect these greens for Momma." I squatted with my back turned and grabbed leaves.

Papa dropped a handful of leaves in my basket. "Forgive me?" He stayed beside me.

"When my wits come back." I scanned the ground for more leaves, purposely avoiding the contrite expression on his face. *Just wait until Momma hears what you did.*

As we neared the fire pit, Momma glared at Papa and rushed to me. "Let me see your eyes." She stared at me while scolding Papa. "Honestly, Michael, I don't know what you were thinking."

"I'm all right." I stepped back and half-smiled. "Papa wants to keep us safe." *Did I just defend him?*

Papa took Momma's hand and whispered, "I had to scare the girls. Their lives may depend on it." He slid an Indian arrow from his rifle sheath.

My heart skipped a beat.

Momma gasped and straightened her back.

"The notched design on the shaft indicates Shawnee. I pulled it from an elk carcass that's no more than two days old. It missed the heart, so the animal bolted. The hunter may have let it go rather than risk being seen." His face remained tense. "We need to keep the flames low and our fire as smokeless as possible from here on out. Let's eat before it gets too dark."

My stomach knotted. *If the Shawnee are ignoring the treaty and coming close to our valley, how much closer are they to the Kentucky settlements? Taking a stand against the Tories back on Indian Creek sounds wiser.*

Momma stepped back, wiping her cheek. She cleared her throat. "Come, children. Time for supper." She used a long stick to spread the burning logs out to cool. "Place your squirrel in the coals."

George handed me a long stick with a skewered squirrel on the end.

"Thank you." I wasn't hungry but needed to be. I joined the others squatting around the fire pit with their sticks. Soon, the stench of searing flesh changed to a succulent roasted aroma. As I ate small bites, my stomach settled.

With a full belly, I leaned back against the tree where Drummer was tied. He soldier-crawled to my side and lay his head in my lap. I stretched out my legs and stared into the blue-green embers flickering inside the fire pit.

Momma stepped to her saddlebag. She removed something, hid it behind her back, and returned. "I have a surprise."

She handed me a leather-bound book with five raised bands on the spine and gold lettering that read *The Vicar of Wakefield*. The gold-tipped pages glinted when I rippled them with my thumb. I smiled at Momma. "When did this come?"

"I had Papa pick it up for the trip a while back. No sense neglecting our reading skills just because we're heading farther into the wilderness. Let's hear the first chapter before it gets too dark. Mary will read first."

I paused from reading to chuckle at the vicar's humorous account of his charitable family and his annoyance with "troublesome guests" overstaying their welcome. His solution for getting rid of them was to loan them something they "would never come back to return."

Papa laughed. "You'll have a greater understanding of this story once we're settled at Fort Boonesborough."

Katie read next, followed by George and Susie. Lizzy concluded the chapter and returned the book to Momma, who nodded. "I heard a few stumbles, but we'll have plenty of practice in the days to come."

What a wonderful distraction from our worries. I grinned until my cheeks hurt.

Papa rolled over what was left of the logs with a long stick, sending tiny sparks a short distance into the dark sky. He returned to his place beside Momma. "We've traveled about sixteen miles today. Good job, children." He gazed at Momma and stroked his chin twice.

I pulled my knees to my chest for comfort. Chin-stroking meant he needed to tell Momma something troubling or wanted her approval for a matter she might not agree with. I'd also noticed the gesture when he left out important information.

Momma frowned at him with a fixed stare.

He met her gaze with soft eyes. "We can't stay on the southbound wagon road to Fort Chiswell."

I sighed, knowing the reason.

"The captain at Wood's Fort said the Boones were delayed in leaving, on account of his wife giving birth.

If we follow the old Cherokee hunter's trail up to the ridgeline and keep our pace, we could reach their place in four or five days."

Momma's eyebrows rose. "I understand the route change. But don't expect a soldier's pace up that rocky buffalo trail. We don't need to worry about catching the Boones. We'll make it just fine—at the children's gait." She stared into the embers.

I turned my head toward the west, expecting to hear the mountains moving ahead of Momma's faith. *How can she be so sure?* My eyes watered.

"Can I help scout for Indian signs?" George's sudden question made me jump.

Papa nodded and stood. "Now, help secure the supplies and off to bed. Morning will be here in a hurry."

We took turns hugging Momma and Papa, then carried armloads of supplies back to the pile for quick loading in the morning. Papa removed the animal debris far into the woods to keep bear and other wild creatures from coming into the camp while we slept.

Momma herded the younger children into the big tent.

George raised one side of the blanket that covered our tent entrance. Katie entered first, followed by Lizzy.

"Thank you." I smiled and reached for the covering so he could go inside.

He shook his head. "No. I should sleep at the entrance."

"And what makes you think so?" I wiggled my head—not about to give up my right to slight evening breezes. "I'm the eldest."

He stood his ground. "I'll help Papa keep watch in case bear or coons come prowling around."

Katie poked her head out and laughed. "Papa doesn't need your help. And besides, the bear would slap you down, bite your neck, and toss you against a tree before you could shoot."

"I'd shoot it dead before it got to me." George leaned toward her, glaring. "If you can do it, so can I."

Katie huffed and retreated to her pallet.

"All right, you can have the entrance tonight; then we'll take turns." I squatted and crawled to the right side, fluffing my limp ticking as George entered.

"Well. I don't want a turn." Katie fluffed her bed. "I don't want to be stolen by Indians while I sleep. They'll get you before a bear does."

"Hush that kind of talk." Lizzy's whine was shrill. "You're scaring me."

Katie huffed. "Don't be a baby. Best to think through these things so you can be prepared to survive."

"You don't have to be mean." I glared.

She shrugged and lay down, turning her face toward the canvas.

I smiled at Lizzy. "We'll have to trust divine protection and Papa." I smoothed my coverings, then felt for rocks and sticks before lying down. "Go to sleep."

I lay on my flat bedroll and breathed the humid air, scented with reeking body odor and turpentine. Maddening chigger bites demanded to be scratched. I listened to night birds, slapped at a mosquito buzzing my ear, and then covered my head with a linen sheet. Katie sighed every time Lizzy squirmed. George started snoring. *It's going to be an impossible night for sleep.*

Instead of counting sheep, all manner of dangerous "what ifs" flitted through my mind. I'd heard of whole families raided and children taken under the cover of night. My stomach knotted. *It's hard to tell my siblings to trust when the Indian threat is real.*

Chapter Four

August 24

Someone jabbed my ribs. I rolled toward my siblings and squinted at a lone beam of sunlight as Lizzy frowned down at me with watery eyes. "George is gone!"

I glanced at his vacant bedding, unconcerned, and cleared the phlegm from my throat. "He's probably checking traps with Papa."

"No." Her voice rose. "Papa ran toward the woods with Drummer, and George wasn't with them. Maybe the Indians took him."

"That Katie." I sighed and sat up, hugging my legs. "Calm down and think it through. Drummer's furious barks would have awakened us if Indians were lurking about."

Katie moaned as she sat up, stretching. "What's wrong?"

"I don't know." I crawled to the tent entrance, landing my left knee on a jagged rock. "Ow!" I hugged my leg and rocked, sucking in shallow breaths.

Momma glanced my way from the fire pit. "What's the matter?"

"A rock." I rubbed my numb leg and stood. "Where's George?"

"Asleep in our tent. Why?"

I shook my head and limped toward her. "Lizzy thought Indians stole him in spite of our watchdog."

Lizzy rushed past me and stood before Momma. "Well, I saw Papa race into the woods with Drummer."

Momma held her belly and stood. "Papa heard rabbits squealing in the traps, is all."

"I knew it was nothing." Katie waggled her head as she stepped beside me.

Momma turned to us with raised eyebrows and hands on hips. She focused on Katie. "George came to our tent last night worried about Indians stealing him. Mind what you say to the younger children. The danger is real. Now, go wake the children and get busy packing the bedrolls and tents."

Katie lowered her head. "Yes, ma'am. I'm sorry."

I made sure Katie saw my smirk before following her. My sympathies were with George. He rarely admitted being afraid.

As we arrived at the big tent, the youngest children poured out and scampered to Momma. George crawled from the entrance and stood up, stretching.

Katie bumped him with her elbow. "You scaredy-cat."

I glared at her. "Stop teasing him, or you'll have to sleep at the entrance tonight. Roll the bedding while George and I pull stakes."

"You don't know what I saw and heard last night." George sneered at Katie, then stomped around to the back side of the tent.

Katie huffed before stooping inside to roll blankets.

I bumped a tent stake loose with the heel of my foot, then wiggled it from the ground opposite George—waiting for him to calm down so I could ask what he saw.

When Katie left with the bedrolls, George stepped around to my side. "Something bumped my arm in the night and grunted. Drummer growled. A standing-up-shadow shuffled through the leaves away from our tents. That's when I got scared and sneaked out to tell Papa. I stood watch while he searched around in the dark, but he didn't find anything. Said it was probably a bear sniffing for food and that he'd check for signs in the morning. Momma told me to stay with them so I wouldn't lay awake and worry all night. I know I didn't imagine it."

As soon as he said bear, my heart fluttered. Memory transported me to the dark ravine at Hans Creek, where I slipped in fresh bear scat on my journey home a week ago.

"Are you all right? You look pale." George touched my shoulder.

My eyes focused on his. I nodded, then breathed again. "I would have been scared too. Wake me next time."

He smiled. "I will. Hope it wasn't an Indian. Is Papa back yet?"

"He's retrieving rabbits." My head throbbed. "Let's get the tent down and packed."

George frowned and mumbled at the ground. "I wanted to go scouting with him. Why didn't he wake me?"

"He must have thought it best to let you sleep." I lifted my corner of the canvas and waited for George to lift his.

As George and I loaded the large canvas on Gideon, Papa entered camp with traps clanking together over his shoulder. He held up a couple of skinned rabbits. Drummer pranced over to me, panting. I sneaked a few scratches under his neck before he lay down in the shade.

Momma stood from the coals. "Well, now we're going to need a fire. Are you sure it's safe?"

Papa nodded and handed the meat to her. "Keep the fire low. Just what's needed for a swift searing. I'll grease these pelts right quick; then we'll eat and get going."

George eased toward Papa, who acknowledged him with a nod. "No signs of Indians this morning. I saw mid-sized bear tracks outside the camp, though. Must have heard Drummer's warning and skedaddled."

George's eyes widened. "It...bumped my arm...could have dragged me out of the tent and...eaten me."

"No—just snooping around. I'll tie Drummer closer to your tent tonight. Help Katie and Lizzy pack the small canvas." Papa turned away, rubbing his chin.

Tiny hairs on the back of my neck prickled, and a shiver went down my spine. *What's he leaving out now?* I rushed to the supplies and retrieved the cast-iron skillet. After placing it on a flat stone in coals to heat, I turned to Momma. "If you can spare me, I'll help Papa with the furs."

Momma's dubious eyes peered up at me as she nodded. *She knows Papa doesn't need help.* I grinned and turned away. *But I have to know the truth.*

Papa had the pelts laid fur-side down on a clean boulder and was rubbing fat pieces over one of the skins, to keep it soft for traveling. If he wondered why I was watching him, he didn't say. *Maybe I shouldn't ask. But I have to.*

Papa greased the other pelt. I took a deep breath. *Now or never.* "What else did you find in the woods?"

He didn't look up. "That William McGuire does a realistic rabbit scream."

I stepped back and gasped.

Papa placed the skin sides together, folded the pelts, and looked at me. "Mr. McGuire handed me these rabbits and said he came across a couple of Cherokee scouts nearby and...well, the way is now clear to the Bluestone River." Papa tied the pelts with sinew and handed them to me, clenching his jaw. "No more questions. Secure these to my saddlebag while I go clean up." He strolled down to the riverbank.

"Yes, sir." *William is safe.* I went to Little Sis, grinning. After tying the pelts on the saddle, I stared into the forest. *Are you still out there, William McGuire? Are you scouting for us?*

I gathered at the shade tree with my family. While Papa prayed, a terrible thought came. *What if it hadn't been a bear sniffing around the tent? What if it was an Indian, and Papa didn't want to alarm us? Drummer's bark scared the Indian away, and then William McGuire killed him.* My stomach churned.

Once everything was cleaned up and repacked, we took hold of our lead ropes and strolled away from New River. My thoughts turned again to William. *Is he following us all the way to Kentucky?* I chuckled. *Of course he isn't.*

The younger children giggled and chattered in front of me for several minutes. Charlie made a game of whacking the bushes we passed with a stick, the same way Papa cleared the brambles ahead of us. When Charlie rested his arm, he sang songs about whacking bears and beasts. Sometimes the words rhymed, but mostly they were redundant and annoying. When we reached the shallow East River, he raced across.

I approached Momma. "May I trade Charlie for Sally? My nerves are fraying already."

She smiled but shook her head. "I'm sorry. Please keep him or trade with Katie. The terrain is steep and will be the remainder of the day. He'll wear down soon enough. Keep your wits about you."

"Yes, ma'am." I waded into the creek, stumbled over fallen branches, and fell into a tangle of briers. I wiped blood from the pricks on my arm and pulled out the tiny thorns. The uneven surface became more jagged, and the ball of my right foot hurt. *Not again.* It had finally healed from my last long walk.

When we stopped to rest, I sat on a log and removed my moccasins to cool my feet. I plucked a few leaves from a bush and stuffed them inside my shoe for more cushion.

Wish I could use the rabbit fur, but we can't afford to waste it. I didn't want to be the first one to suggest riding after only an hour's walk.

"My feet hurt. I want to ride." Nancy protested first.

"I'll ride with her." Lizzy beat me to the offer.

Momma chuckled. "We're all ready to ride. Too late to change our minds about Kentucky, I suppose?" She smiled at Papa.

Papa grinned. "Yes, ma'am. But we need to consider the horses before ourselves. We'll take a lunch break once we reach the summit. Let's go."

I sighed, put my moccasins back on, and rushed to speak to Papa. "Is Mr. McGuire scouting for us? Is he coming to Kentucky?"

Papa's eyebrows rose. "No. He's on his way back to Cook's Fort."

I leaned closer. "Was it actually an Indian that touched George?"

"What? No." Papa frowned and shook his head. "It was a black bear. I promise." He sighed. "Stop making things up to worry about. Now, get. I have to concentrate."

I smiled and went to check Rebel's feet. Having a bear nudge George in the night was better than worrying about an Indian being so bold.

After an exhausting two hours, with a brief rest in between, we arrived at the summit. Papa released his horse to graze and turned to us. "Stay quiet until I return."

"Can I come?" George whispered.

"No. You scout around here. I'll be back." He sounded anxious.

My stomach fluttered as Papa disappeared around the bend. Despite his denial, I imagined William out there watching after us and felt safe.

George walked General to a patch of grass and examined the bank for tracks.

I chuckled as he tried to walk like Papa, examining the ground up and down the bank, looking for broken twigs, shoe prints, or recent markings on trees.

"No signs of Indians." George returned, puffing out his chest.

Papa rushed back from a different direction from where he started. "All clear, but we'll eat a hurried bite and move on." His lips were pressed together as he stood beside Momma.

If the way is clear, why the rush? Why not let us ride the blame horses awhile? I knew the horses couldn't handle our weight, but complaining helped. I blew out a breath and joined the family, circling around Momma for our divvy of jerky.

Sitting on the rocky ground seemed futile for such a short time, but took the pressure off my tender foot.

When I glanced at Momma, my heart pricked. She leaned back on one hand while holding her stomach with the other, and then she rocked forward and released a sigh before standing. Her face dropped. "Shall we go?"

She must be exhausted. Why am I complaining about rocks and a sore foot?

Sally planted herself in front of Momma, gripping her petticoat and whimpering. "Up."

Momma took her hand and looked down. "You must be a big girl. I can't carry you."

The sniffling toddler stepped forward, and Momma gave a gentle tug for her to catch up. *Poor Momma. That must have been hard. Sally isn't a big girl. Maybe Papa will allow a longer rest at the next stop.*

I sighed, took Rebel's rope, and moved forward, holding out my other hand to Charlie.

"Go home." Charlie pooched out his lips and stamped his foot.

"Sorry, little man." Papa lifted him onto his shoulders and walked ahead. "We're on an adventure. We'll have a new home in Kentucky, and someday I'll take you hunting like George. But you can't fuss about traveling and camping."

Charlie smiled and nodded. Before reaching a low-hanging tree branch, Papa flipped him overhead and back to the ground. "Go to Mary now."

He refused to hold my hand but kept in step for the better part of an hour. When we stopped, Papa only allowed enough time for us to relieve ourselves in the bushes while he checked the horses.

As the afternoon heat became unbearable, Charlie tripped over a tree root and landed on his forearms with an "Hmph." I stooped to help him up, but he stood, shaking his head and brushing off dirt. "No cry." With a half-smile, he reached for my hand.

I felt a squeeze in my chest. "You're getting so big." My eyes watered.

He beamed up at me and jutted out his chest as he marched away like a little soldier.

Our shade diminished with the tree line as the path became rocky and steep. Sweat trickled down my neck, and my undergarments were soaked. Sips of water only made my thirst more intense. My now-raw foot radiated heat as if I were walking through white-hot coals. I wanted to sit down and cry.

I need to tend to this. Papa's battle story of Shawnee Chief Cornstalk came to mind. The chief had shouted, "Be strong" to his braves to rally them. Even Joshua shouted it to the Israelites in the Bible story. I stood still, closed my eyes, and shouted as loud as I could, "Be strong."

A few giggles followed. Papa smiled and nodded, then held a finger to his lips. Silent misery returned.

We made a slight descent toward a shallow creek in a clearing with good grass for the horses. I peered at Papa. *Please, say we're camping here for the night.*

"Wait here while George and I check the perimeter." The two strode away.

Sally whined as her bowels made a gurgling sound, followed by a foul stench.

"This can't wait." Momma lifted her and ran toward the creek. She dashed past Papa and stripped off Sally's soiled clothes. Sally sat in the water, bawling.

Tears of concern for my baby sister wet my cheeks as Momma cuddled and rocked her. *We must stop and rest.*

Papa waved the rest of us down. I led Rebel to graze and loosened his girth. "Maybe we'll make camp, and I can free you from this load." I rubbed my hand down his sweaty legs, feeling for sores or swelling, then scratched behind his ear. "Good boy."

I left him and joined Charlie and my sisters, abandoning our outer garments on the bank. I plopped down in the creek, upstream from Sally. Every part of my body ached. I splashed the cool rippling water over me, and the pain in my foot eased. *Please, God. Allow us to rest here.*

Momma wrapped her apron around Sally and carried her to a small cluster of bushes, where the only shade existed. She waved her hand for us to come. Her brow furrowed, and her lips formed a straight line as she handed out bear jerky and hard tack.

"The area is safe." George returned ahead of Papa. He sat, stretching his legs in front of him, and sighed as Momma gave him jerky. "Thank you, Momma."

Papa strolled in and sat cross-legged beside Momma. "We'll rest a minute longer, then head up that mountain trail." He pointed. "Should take an hour. We'll make camp when we reach the plateau."

I sighed at the steep grade looming ahead of us. The trail disappeared as it twisted around trees and boulders. The mountain seemed to rise into the misty clouds, and my willingness to conquer it waned.

Momma faced Papa with narrowed eyes. "I'm exhausted. The children are weakening, and Sally's bowels are ailing. I need to mix a remedy for her. She also has some infected chigger bites from her scratching. We need to make camp here."

Papa shook his head. "We must make it up that mountain before dark. We're too close to the Wagon Road."

That's why he's been so antsy.

"Just one more hour. Then we'll be off the main route and confound our pursuers. I'll put Sally on the horse."

"No, sir!" Momma stepped back with her hands on her hips.

My jaw dropped. Rarely did Momma defy Papa with such a tone.

She stood her ground. "For the sake of the children—we stop here and trust our God."

Papa's nostrils flared as he pointed. "We make it up that mountain to safety before nightfall. If we wait until morning, we risk being seen going that away and won't escape. We may as well head back to Wood's Fort and pray they can protect me from being captured and hanged."

The long silent stare between them knotted my stomach. Tears dribbled down Momma's checks. "We go back then." Her voice cracked.

"So be it." Papa shook his head and turned away with long strides toward Little Sis. He untied the tent bundles and let them fall to the ground.

My heart raced. Sally's limpness, Charlie's quietness, and Momma's disturbing emotional state convinced me her choice was the correct one.

Maybe Papa should just go into hiding with the McGuires. I went in search of a remedy for my foot.

Chapter Five

August 25

"Wake up, but stay quiet." Papa hunched at the tent entrance. Moonlight shone on his back. "Roll your bedding. We have to leave—now."

I bolted from my pallet, smoothed the covers, and then rolled my bedding as comprehension came. George scrambled out of the tent ahead of me. I hurried to Rebel, secured the bedroll behind the saddle, and turned to search for Momma.

Susie and Nancy sat dazed in the middle of camp, holding the whimpering Sally and Charlie. Momma emerged from the big tent with an armful of blankets as the tent collapsed behind her. My step forward made her jump.

"Land sakes!" She shook her head.

"Sorry I scared you. What's happening?" I took one of the pallets from her arms and waited.

Momma leaned toward me, whispering. "Papa scouted in the night. Tories are camped two hours back the way we came. We must get over that mountain by daybreak."

She stepped away, but I grabbed her arm. "What about Sally?"

"The remedy calmed her bowels. She'll be fine. We'll eat later." Momma moved toward the horses.

My heart raced as I led Rebel to a moonlit clearing and finished loading. I tugged on his saddle and bedroll, then joined my siblings to wait on the others.

"Do you know what's going on yet?" Katie yawned and sat beside me.

The wide-eyed children studied my face. I half-smiled to keep them calm. "Momma's changed her mind about going back to Wood's Fort. Papa wants to get an early start up the mountain before it gets too hot." I leaned toward Katie's ear. "All I can say. They're already scared."

Two figures appeared in the shadows and moved forward. I clutched at my throat and gasped. George and Papa stepped into the light, and I released my breath but felt dizzy.

Papa knelt on one knee in front of us. "We can't go back to Wood's Fort. I need you to be strong, brave, and quiet as we head up the mountain in the dark. Charlie and Sally will ride until daybreak."

Momma stepped forward. "Sally can't hold on by herself."

"Nancy can ride and hold her. Bring your horse." Papa lifted Nancy into his arms and waited while Momma retrieved Sir.

Papa placed Nancy on the saddle and then hoisted Sally in front of her. His hand caressed Momma's back. "They'll be fine. This is safer and faster. Nancy won't let Sally fall. I can tie Sally's ankles with a long strip of cloth under the horse's belly if you want. But she'll be happier swinging them."

"I won't let her fall, Momma." Nancy sat tall. "I'm strong enough."

Momma tilted her head toward the stars as if praying, then released a soft sigh.

I hoisted Charlie onto Rebel. "Hold tight. You're riding without me." He grinned, and I glanced into the hazy glow above the trees. *Amen to whatever Momma prayed.*

"Stay close to each other. Let's go." Papa hawed Gideon and Little Sis as he stepped away with Drummer prancing behind him.

Charlie squeezed the pommel of the saddle with both hands. I waited until George's horse was a few paces ahead, sucked in a deep breath, and followed him up the winding mountain trail.

The worst part about being awake in a dark forest isn't the scary sounds of creaking tree limbs, noisy night creatures, or unseen prowlers, but my imagination. What if we come upon sleeping Indians? What if there are rattlesnakes among these boulders? What if a cougar jumps down on us? What if—

Loud splashes accompanied my stumbling across a shallow creek. Rebel halted, and Charlie whimpered. I kicked a tree root with my sore foot as I neared the bank. "Tarnation" shot out of my mouth. I rubbed the throbbing digit, then grasped Rebel's rope. "Wish I had your eyesight."

Charlie giggled and whispered, "Tarnation. Tarnation."

"No. That's not a good word." I glanced back at him. "Momma won't like it. Be quiet now and listen to the birds waking up."

As I limped along the rocky trail, my ears rang with the high pitches of cicada, crickets, and frogs. Almost an hour later, the chirps of night birds merged with the songs of morning birds, and the dark-purple sky swirled into the morning gray.

When Papa stopped in a clearing on top of the mountain, we circled the horses around him. His slight smile raised my spirits. "Good job, family. We can take time to eat and rest in this refreshing breeze for a while."

Momma removed three pouches from her saddlebags. "Along with jerky, I want everyone to eat at least one handful of dried carrots and peas to prevent impaction. This is where all our hard work of gardening pays off."

She peered at Papa. "May we enjoy story time after we eat? I think there's enough light here."

"We can take a two-chapter break to lighten our moods." He wrapped his arm around Momma's waist and pulled her into a hug.

Glad they made up. I sighed and sat cross-legged with my siblings and took a bite of jerky.

Papa stepped back and smiled at us while he sat. "After seeing those Tories last night, I sneaked down to the main road, followed it a far piece until I came to a creek. I waded some distance before climbing the bank and hurrying back to our camp. Their hounds will follow the scent I made down the main road to that creek and then be confused. That oughta be the end of the pursuit. The Tories know the frontier forts are manned by Patriot militia."

His use of "oughta be" wasn't reassuring.

After my last bite of sweet bear jerky, I wiped my hands on my dingy apron and retrieved the book. We took turns reading the second and third chapters about the vicar's arrogance and the theft of his entire fortune. I sighed and closed the book. "How could that girl's papa be so cruel and forbid the marriage—just because the vicar lost his fortune? And I don't like the vicar's wife and daughters. They're too uppity."

Papa laughed, but Momma stared at the ground, frowning.

I handed her the book. "What's wrong?"

She raised her head with watery eyes. "I've wished for finer things, such as what the vicar's family had. Now, here we are in the same predicament."

"What do you mean?" I frowned.

"I didn't appreciate what we had. Now, all we have are the bare essentials needed to survive this trip and start over in Kentucky." She touched Papa's hand. "Have I been as spoiled as the vicar's wife?"

"Not hardly." Papa's head tilted back as he chuckled. "We have one more hour-long hard climb. Then it's an easy descent to the Muellers' cabin. I met Mr. Mueller a while back, and he offered us a place to stay if we came this way."

"With straw beds?" I squealed.

He nodded, then stroked his chin as he peered at Momma. "Yes, and two young men who'll probably take a fancy to you and Katie."

Momma's eyes widened.

My excitement over straw beds waned as my stomach knotted. *Men scare me.*

He shrugged. "But it will be a safe place to rest and regroup. Sally and Charlie have to walk now. The incline is too steep."

Katie grinned at me. "Why would they fancy us?"

I shook my head. "I don't know, but I'm not interested in being gawked at." *I'm sure my appearance is horrid.*

Papa stood and helped Momma up, wrapping her in his arms. "I hope to give you fine things once we're settled again."

She smiled. "Then we should get going. Sooner we get to Kentucky, the sooner we'll have a roof over our heads."

Papa kissed Momma's lips longer than he usually did in front of us. I grinned and looked away. The children giggled. George strolled to his horse.

"I hope to have a beau someday." Katie grinned and hugged herself.

Lizzy gave her a shove, giggling. "You? With a beau? You're too mean."

I laughed so hard my belly hurt. *I want a beau someday too, but Lizzy would say I'm too bossy.*

Susie and Nancy held Charlie's hand until they all slipped on the loose rocks and fell in a heap before sliding a foot back down. Charlie sniffled and wiped off his knees. The girls shook dust from their petticoats.

After checking on them, Momma placed her hands on the ground with her rump in the air. "You'll have to crawl and climb individually, like this." She demonstrated to the giggling children, and we all followed suit.

"Oui-shi-cat-to-oui." George shouted Chief Cornstalk's rally.

Rebel followed beside me as I crawled with my rump in the air, imagining what a sight we'd be to scouts or Indian braves. *The wild creatures in the forest must be frightened.*

It didn't take long for my body to complain. I gritted my teeth, enduring the throbbing pain in my foot as we inched our way up the rocky incline. Loose rock made Rebel stumble, then stop. I rose and rubbed his neck. "Sorry, boy. We'll reach the top soon and rest."

I peered at the grassy rolling hills of New River Valley behind us. *A lot of memories in a year and a half.* As I turned to the trail ahead, Momma's feet slipped out from under her. She landed on her knees and slid a few feet before flipping over to sit.

"How bad are you hurt?" I rushed to her.

She lifted her petticoat, revealing scraped and bloody knees.

"Momma fell," George shouted.

Papa started back down, but Momma waved him on. "I'm all right. Just scrapes. Keep going." She stood, dabbing the wounds with her petticoat.

Sally sobbed and reached around Momma's legs. "Hold you."

"I can't pick you up." Momma patted the child's back. "Let's keep going so we can rest again."

"Oui-shi-cat-to-oui." The shout came from Papa. "We're almost there. You can do it."

My back ached from hunching over for so long on the climb, but I didn't feel pain in my foot anymore. I didn't know if that was good or bad. Excited whoops from my siblings, who'd reached the summit, spurred me on.

Papa stood before a shallow creek a few feet away, shading his eyes with his hand. "This is the Bluestone River." He turned to us. "Good place to rest and cool off. We'll head down when Momma's ready."

Sally rushed to Momma. "Wait, baby. I'll hold you in a minute. Let me sit down and tend to my knees." She retrieved the pouch of salve and bandages from her saddlebag and sat on the ground.

Nancy ran to the bank, shaking her head as she peered into the water. "It's not blue, and why is it called a river when it looks like a creek?"

Papa laughed on his way to Momma with a canteen. "It becomes a large river downstream to the northeast. Look for shades of blue-gray limestone along the bank."

Susie and Nancy went in search of blue stones, and Papa squatted in front of Momma. "Let me see your knees."

She raised her petticoat, and he and I winced at the same time. Her knees were bruised and swollen with abrasions and caked with dried blood. Momma drank from the canteen and then doused one of the bandages. Papa sat beside her, and Sally plopped in his lap.

"Blue rocks." Nancy squealed seconds later.

"Come, Charlie." I took his hand and went to Momma. "He needs salve on his scrapes, too."

Charlie pulled away, frowning. "No. Burn."

"I'll blow on it." I placed him beside Papa, wet a bandage, and blew on his knee as I cleaned and treated it with the ointment.

Now me. I took the pouch over to Sir as if I were going to put it away, but then removed some bandages and sneaked to the stream without limping. *I'll tend to it myself. No need to trouble Momma.* I removed my moccasins and eased my sore foot into the cool water. After treating the wound, I folded a bandage, placed it in the shoe, and stood. The cushion worked. *I can do this.* I smiled and joined the family.

Katie and Lizzy had tied a quilt between the saddles of Rusty and Patriot and made a nice, shady place to rest. I stooped, then plopped down inside. "Good idea."

"You're a 'troublesome guest of bad character' just like the vicar said." Katie glared. "Here—take my best leaf fan and go away."

Lizzy giggled, but Katie narrowed her eyes.

Stunned, I took the hickory leaf fan and went to Momma's blanket, stewing on hurt feelings as I fanned my face. *Guess it was rude not to ask first.* I sighed, then chuckled. *The vicar's advice worked though—nice fan.*

Momma glanced at me, then at Papa. "Shall we go? I'm looking forward to meeting the Muellers."

Papa rose and lifted Momma by her hands. She cringed as she stood.

The excitement of sleeping on a cabin floor overruled my fear of gawking men. I lifted Rebel's rope and waited for Katie. Handing her the fan, I curtsied. "Thank you, kind miss."

Katie's head wobbled. "Use manners next time, and you might be invited to share our shade."

I curtsied again and smirked. *Maybe I should try being nicer. But I'm used to being bossy.*

Chapter Six

As we descended the mountain, our trail wound through stubby trees. After we crossed a small creek, the path turned westerly and widened into a grassy clearing with wagon ruts.

I smiled at a two-story white-stone cottage, much like those I'd seen as a little girl in the Shenandoah Valley before we crossed the Allegheny Mountains. The largest barn I'd ever seen cast a shadow on the home. *How long have they been settled here to have such a wonderful place?*

A small yapping dog alerted a plump woman who was tending cooking pots in the yard. Drummer growled, with bristled fur, until Papa looked at him and he hushed. The other dog lay back down.

"Velkome, velkome," the woman shouted with a heavy German accent and waved. She stepped forward, scanning us as we neared. "Pleasure to greet you." She smiled at Momma.

Papa removed his hat. "Thank you. I'm Michael Shirley, and I present my wife, Katherine."

Mrs. Mueller nodded. "I'm Matilda Mueller. Please, come. We have plenty of stew for lunch."

"*Dankeschon.*" Momma thanked her in German.

Mrs. Mueller grinned as she gushed into full boisterous German about how wonderful it was to have guests who were German and how lonely she had been for the company of other women.

Momma released Sir's rope, motioned for Susie and Nancy to come, then took Sally's and Charlie's hands and followed Mrs. Mueller to the cottage.

Papa removed the rabbit furs from his pack on Little Sis as the rest of us waited for instruction.

A white-bearded man emerged from the barn, followed by two muscular young men carrying wooden buckets. They were the same height, with long blond hair plaited down their backs. My eyes remained fixed in wonder. These handsome men had identical faces with square jaws.

With my heart turning flips, I eased behind Rebel's neck to hide my staring. I'd never seen twins before, and these were especially alluring. I grinned and watched them stroll toward us with the older man. When they smiled at the same time and nodded at me with intense blue eyes, my breath caught.

Katie shoved my arm.

"What?" I continued to stare.

"You're gawking at those men."

My cheeks burned. I nodded and grinned. "They're pleasing to the eye. Don't you agree?"

Katie giggled.

"Hallo," the older man greeted in German as he neared and glanced at us. His sons shook hands with Papa first and stepped back.

Papa reached out to Mr. Mueller next. "Hallo, Hans. Good to see you again. We'd like to take you up on your offer to stay overnight."

"*Ja*, and you are velcome, Mr. Shirley." After the handshake, Mr. Mueller shook his head and frowned. "You are going to Kentucky settlement with your family—alone?" He spoke in German, but I understood everything he said.

I stroked Rebel's sweaty neck and listened.

Papa responded in German. "Trying to catch the Boones in five days. Want to get in on the best land claims before spring. We'll camp at the new posts along the Clinch River."

Mr. Mueller shook his head and turned to me, pointing to the barn. "Please, take horses. My sons, Hans and Fredrick, will help." He ushered his sons forward. "Help these children. We'll come in a moment."

Papa raised the pelts. "Please accept these furs as partial payment for our lodging."

Mr. Mueller nodded, and one of the twins took them and Little Sis's rope.

Papa glanced at me. "Take Drummer with you. Tether him with the horses." He took a few steps away with Mr. Mueller.

As the other twin reached for Rebel, I shook my head. *"Nien. Dankeschon..."* My face flushed as I lost my nerve to continue in German. "I'll bring him."

He tilted his head and frowned, then moved on to Momma's horse.

As everyone left, I ran my hand down Rebel's leg to stall and eavesdrop. Mr. Mueller spoke. "You're mighty brave, Mr. Shirley, but foolish. Not good to risk your family due to impatience. Families a few miles south were raided a month ago. Best to wait here for others."

Raids? I stood too fast and had to lean my dizzy head on Rebel's shoulder.

"Get on to the barn, Mary." Papa sounded stern.

With a slight shove, I stayed beside Rebel and moved toward the barn, but peered back.

Papa pointed.

As I focused on the barn, fear crept in. *Maybe we should wait.*

When I arrived, George met me. "I'll take him. Momma said I can stay and help Hans and Fredrick in the barn.

You have to wash up over there and go inside." He pointed to an area surrounded by various yellow and blue flowers.

I handed him Rebel's lead and glanced toward the barn. One of the twins tipped his hat and stepped back out of sight.

Having men around to take over the horse grooming made me feel somewhat uppity. I went to the floral-scented spring, splashed water on my face, and washed my hands with a sliver of lye soap that had been left on a stone. I dried my hands on the linen towel draped over a small drying rack.

Staying here with extra men for protection makes good sense and suits me just fine.

I admired the gray-blue stones in the steps as I climbed onto a whitewashed porch. Rectangular planks in the door were carved with swirled ivy vines. It opened without squeaks into a whimsical space full of lively blues, reds, and yellows, offset by whitewashed log walls. Aromas of venison stew and fresh baked bread made my stomach gurgle as I glanced around, lightheaded.

A walled staircase, with post rails on one side, ascended to the second story behind a beautiful smooth and shiny table. To the right of the main area were two separate rooms with doors. My cheeks were fatigued from smiling so wide, but I couldn't stop. *I could stay here forever— I just have to decide which twin to marry.* The thought shocked me. *Have I become like the vicar's daughter Olivia, so desirous of "fine trappings" that I would become flirtatious and vain?*

"Velkome." Mrs. Mueller smiled beside a walnut counter and spoke English to me. "Your momma and sisters are arranging bedding in the loft. Come. Please, carry this platter to the table."

"Yes, ma'am." I set the platter of sliced, buttered bread on the table, too nervous to try my German again. "Thank you for allowing us to stay here. What a wonderful home you have."

She beamed a smile at me. "*Nein.* I'm pleased to have company of such sweet family."

I was still grinning when the door opened and all the men entered. Papa and Mr. Mueller didn't seem at odds anymore. The twin across from me smiled back. I looked away, embarrassed. *He thinks I'm smiling at him.*

Momma limped a little as she and my sisters clamored down the loft stairs, grinning. We gathered around the large table. Mr. Mueller prayed a blessing in German for our travel safety, and then Mrs. Mueller served our bowls with a hearty venison stew.

The twin glanced at me every few seconds while we ate, and I pretended not to notice between peeks of my own. When Papa and Mr. Mueller excused themselves from the table, my attention followed them.

They moved to a sitting area in the far corner and unrolled a map. Mr. Mueller pointed to a location. I couldn't hear the conversation over Mrs. Mueller's loud, animated story to Momma about her trip from Philadelphia.

I watched Papa. Sometimes he looked worried and stroked his chin. Other times, he smiled and nodded his head. I didn't know whether to be worried or not.

During a lull in Mrs. Mueller's story, the other twin bumped George. "Let's go to the porch and clean our guns."

Momma smiled and gave George a nod. He jumped up, beaming, grabbed his and Papa's rifles, and followed the twins outside.

A fingernail tapping on the table drew my attention back to Momma. She pointed to Sally, who was asleep in her lap, and glanced toward the loft stairs. I bumped Katie to bring Charlie, who was bobbing his head on the table. I lifted Sally and carried her upstairs.

The loft was full of straw-stuffed pallets covered with white linen coverlets, but instead of smelling like hay, the room smelled of cedar with wafts of sweetness. A bundle of blue, pink, and yellow wildflowers, with cedar twigs mixed in, hung from a rafter near the small, opened porthole.

I laid Sally down and stood with my eyes closed, sniffing the air, then peered at Katie. "Am I like Olivia?"

Katie stood in front of Charlie's pallet, staring at me with raised eyebrows, as if afraid to answer.

I grinned. "I won't be mad. Tell me the truth."

She glanced at her feet first and then back to me with a smile. "I was going to ask you the same thing—about me. I could be happy here forever."

"If we marry the twins, you'll be my sister-in-law, as well as my sister." I laughed.

Katie didn't smile. Her brow furrowed. "We need a good reason to go outside and talk to them."

"Momma needs fresh plantain for her knees." I smiled and eased toward the stairs.

"Yes. She does." Katie giggled and followed me down.

Momma and Mrs. Mueller were washing dishes. Lizzy, Susie, and Nancy were drying and putting away.

"Come help." Momma held out a towel.

My heart raced. "Will you need fresh plantain for the cuts on your knees?"

Katie smiled.

"You have injuries?" Mrs. Mueller lifted Momma's skirt. "Yes. Plantain is good. We have at the creek."

Momma's eyes widened. She glanced at Papa, then at me and Katie. "I will allow you to go, but hurry."

Katie and I bounced out the door and turned toward the twins. They jumped to their feet, and George stood but frowned at us.

My tongue stuck to the roof of my mouth, and my stomach fluttered. I turned my head toward Katie. *I can't do it.*

She stepped forward. "We need to gather fresh plantain at the creek for our injuries. Do we need protecting?"

What boldness. I smiled.

"Yes," one of the twins said. "The creek is secluded."

The other grabbed his gun and looked at George. "Do you mind finishing without us?"

"No." George frowned at me. "My sisters don't need help. They know how to shoot. Why, Katie shot a bear once, and Mary's killed a cougar."

The twin closest to Katie grinned. "You don't say? Well, we're closer to Indians out here. We can't let them go alone and risk being captured."

George shook his head.

"Momma approved." I moved down the steps behind the twins. "Now hush and clean the guns."

Katie followed me down, but rushed ahead. "What are your names, and how does one know the difference between you?"

I shook my head. *She is much braver than I.*

The one on her right turned with a smile. "I'm Fredrick. He's Hans. I have a mole above my eyebrow, which makes me the handsome one." He stepped around Katie and offered his right arm.

Katie placed her hand on top.

My jaw dropped. *What is she doing? We aren't allowed to be escorted without Papa's permission.*

Before I could correct her, Hans handed me a basket and poked his right elbow toward me. I shook my head and stepped back with my heart pounding. He withdrew his arm.

As I walked beside Hans, Drummer whimpered from the corral, where he watched me from on the tether line. *Sorry, boy.*

Hans cleared his throat. "I hope your papa accepts my papa's offer to settle here instead of Kentucky."

I stopped mid-stride and faced him. "What offer?"

The corner of his mouth curved into a sheepish grin. "My papa wants to start a dairy and will give your papa land to stay here and partner with him. I want to ask your papa about marrying you." Hans took my hand to his lips and kissed it.

I jerked my hand back and shook my head. "I'm only thirteen, and Katie is twelve. Papa won't let us have suitors until we're fifteen."

Hans cleared his throat and glanced at his feet. "I'm...sorry. I thought you were...older. Fredrick and I just turned eighteen. Maybe, once the war is over and the Indians make peace again, I'll come to Kentucky and find you. Would you consider me if I do?" The softness of his gaze made my legs feel wobbly.

I smiled, then shook off the stupor. "One can't make promises so far in the future. And besides, you just met me. Why would you want to wait on a scrawny little girl like me?"

He turned toward the trail, holding his arm out to me again. "Because. You intrigue me with your independent manner, and I think you're beautiful."

My cheeks felt hot. I glanced back at the cottage, making sure Papa wasn't watching as I took his arm.

He chuckled and lay his free hand on mine. As we walked, the sore on my foot renewed its presence, but I willed myself not to limp. *I can't appear weak now.*

Chapter Seven

Fredrick held Katie's forearms as she peered into his eyes, smiling.

My breath caught. I let go of Hans and stood still.

Fredrick released her and spun around on his heels, glancing first at me, then the ground. Katie reached for the basket without acknowledging me.

"I'll get that, my lady." Fredrick bowed like a lord, and Katie giggled.

I flushed with a mixture of shock and anger. *What does she think she's doing?*

Hans took my basket and went to his brother. He grabbed Fredrick's sleeve and pulled him away from Katie and toward a patch of plantain leaves.

I glared at Katie. "Come here."

"No. I'm going to pick leaves." She pranced to where the twins were working and continued to act giddy around Fredrick.

My jaw dropped. *She is flirtatious, like Olivia. I'll have to tell Momma.*

Fredrick said something to Katie that made her frown as he handed her the full basket. She flipped her braid before stomping toward me with squinting, wet eyes.

"Don't talk to me." She wiped her cheeks as she passed and headed back to the cabin.

I can't believe her behavior.

Fredrick removed his hat and watched his feet as he approached. "I'm sorry. It was just a peck. Hans and I don't want trouble with your papa. Must you tell him?"

They kissed? I shook my head at Fredrick. "I won't say anything to Papa." *But Katie will get an earful from Momma. I must tell her.* My chest hurt more than my foot as I anticipated her reaction.

Fredrick sighed. "Thank you. Hans and I are...want to be honorable men."

Hans stepped beside Fredrick and handed me the basket.

I half-smiled. "Thank you."

"Let's get back." Hans led the way.

As we entered the yard, Katie was stirring a large iron pot over the fire pit. Mrs. Mueller stood beside her, chatting until she saw me. "Pour your leaves here."

Katie glanced up, then back at the kettle.

Fredrick tipped his hat. "See you later. We have chores in the barn. You coming, Hans?"

"I'll carry in fresh water first." Hans took the water bucket toward the spring.

I looked at the porch. "Where's George?"

"With the papas, checking on traps." Mrs. Mueller lifted the steaming, limp leaves from the pot with her ladle.

My breath caught. *Did they see Katie and Fredrick?*

Susie shouted, "Come see the puppies," from a pile of logs nearby. Lizzy sat among them, feeding the momma dog a piece of jerky.

I shook my head on my way up the steps. *What am I going to tell Momma?*

Hans followed me inside with the bucket and placed it on the small round table near the door. He filled a gourd dipper and offered me the first drink.

"No, thank you." I glanced around the room. *Where's Momma?*

My eyes fell back on Hans as he drank. Water dribbled from the corner of his mouth, down his chin, then past his bobbing Adam's apple. It trickled beyond his unfastened collar and through the maze of curly blond chest hairs that peeked out of his linen shirt.

Breathe. My heart raced. *What is this feeling?*

He hung the dipper back on the peg and tilted his head at me. "Are you all right?"

I drew a deep breath and nodded.

"I have to get to the barn. See you later." He waited.

I couldn't answer.

He chuckled, tipped his hat, and crossed the threshold, shaking his head.

He must think I'm a dummkopf.

I swallowed hard and watched him stride to the barn.

"Ah, you're back." Momma's voice made me jump and hold my chest, feeling ashamed but not sure why.

She hobbled down the stairs. "Where's Katie?"

I tilted my head toward the door. "Helping Mrs. Mueller steep leaves."

Momma's brows furrowed. "Call her in, please."

My lips numbed as I stepped onto the porch. *Does she already know what happened? Deep breath.* "Katie...Momma wants you."

Her glare seared a hole in my heart as she passed me and entered the cottage. *She thinks I tattled.*

Katie dropped to her knees in front of Momma. "I'm sorry. It happened so fast...I didn't mean to."

Momma's head cocked to one side. "What are you talking about?"

I held my breath. *She doesn't know.*

"The kiss." Katie sniffled and glanced at me, then back to Momma, as if realizing her blunder.

Momma plopped into the closest chair. "Explain yourself."

After a loud sigh, Katie sat cross-legged on the floor, wiping her face with her apron. Watching her squirm made my belly hurt. I wanted to go to her.

She sniffled one more time and stood. Her back straightened, but her expression remained contrite, as if ready to face the consequences. When she took a deep breath, so did I.

"I let Fredrick kiss me when we went to the creek."

Momma gasped. Her eyes widened.

Mrs. Mueller entered with a bowlful of steeped plantain and placed it on the table near Momma, along with a stack of four-inch-square linen bandages.

I glanced at Momma, who took a deep breath.

Mrs. Mueller took a stepped back, observing Katie. "Are you ill, child?"

Katie shook her head. "A little queasy at the moment."

"Ah, I'll mix you something." Mrs. Mueller scurried to a beautiful walnut cabinet indented with dotted swirls and removed a clay pot from its top shelf.

"No, please, Matilda, she just needs to go upstairs and lie down for a bit." Momma's head remained still, but her eyes looked at Katie and then the staircase.

Katie blew her nose into her apron and stooped toward Momma, kissing her cheek and whispering, "I'm sorry."

Momma nodded. "I'll be up later."

Katie trudged up the stairs.

Poor Katie. How wretched she must feel. And she's yet to face Papa.

Mrs. Mueller shrugged and brought a smaller container. "This salve is good for wounds, burns, and blisters. We mix it with the leaves."

Momma stared at the loft stairs a moment more and then turned her attention to Mrs. Mueller, who had sat down beside her.

Mrs. Mueller crushed leaves with a wooded pestle, then stirred in some of her salve. After dabbing a handful of bandages into the slimy green soup, she handed them to Momma, who winced as she stuck them to her wounds.

"Wrap the strips around her knees and tie off the ends." Mrs. Mueller pointed to the pile of dry bandages.

When they weren't looking, I slipped a few bandage squares into my apron pocket. *No need to worry Momma. I'll sneak down after everyone's asleep and use Mrs. Mueller's salve on my wound.*

Momma sat back in the chair while I bandaged her knees.

Mrs. Mueller cleared the table and then stepped to the doorjamb. "Ah, the men are back with meat. Now, you rest." She glanced back at Momma. "Your big girl can help me prepare game for supper." She bounded outside.

Momma took my hand. Her face drooped, and her eyes watered. "Did you see Katie with Fredrick?"

"Yes." I gulped. "But not the kiss. Fredrick let go of her arms as Hans and I arrived. They thought Katie, and I were older. Fredrick apologized. Must you tell Papa?"

Momma looked to the ceiling with a sigh. "I'm not sure what to do." She eased out of the chair and climbed the stairs. I wanted to be the fly that followed her up, but Mrs. Mueller needed my help.

Papa entered a second later. "Where's Momma?" He didn't seem upset.

"Upstairs." I held my breath as Papa clomped to the loft.

Staying busy is best. I rushed into the yard and helped Mrs. Mueller skewer rabbits. As we hung them above the fire pit, Sally, Nancy, and Charlie ran out of the house, followed by Papa.

He smiled at Mrs. Mueller. "We wish to work out a barter for our stay and food. I'll work out the details with your husband."

They didn't talk about Katie?

"*Ja,* you talk to Hans. He will tell you *nein* better than I."

Papa laughed and walked toward the barn, where the Mueller men and George stood talking. Papa spoke to Mr. Mueller and offered his hand, but the elderly man shook his head and refused to shake. I smiled. *Mrs. Mueller was correct.* The men led the boys toward the cottage.

I stepped onto the porch and waved to Hans Junior with a smile as he entered the yard, but turned away in fear of Papa catching me. My heart fluttered.

"Do I need to have a talk with you as well?" Momma stood in the doorjamb with her hands on her hips.

I gulped and looked down at the whitewashed boards. "No, ma'am."

Momma lifted my chin and gazed into my eyes. "We'll encounter many men as we pass through forts and small blockades on the way to Fort Boonesborough. You know what is proper. But I warn you as I did Katie—guard your heart."

"Yes, ma'am."

She released me and stepped back inside.

It's too late. My heart is already stolen.

Nonetheless, I heeded Momma's warning and ignored Hans's repeated glances throughout supper, hoping he'd understand.

When Hans finished eating, he laid his fork down and scooted his chair away from the table. "Excuse me. I must say good night." He nodded at me and departed to the room he shared with Fredrick.

My chest ached. "May I turn in now as well?"

Papa nodded and continued listening to Mr. Mueller's dairy farm plans.

I escaped to the privacy of the loft with my eyes watering. *What does "guard your heart" mean, anyway? I like Hans. I want to smile at him and know what a kiss feels like.*

I lay on a pallet, pleased to sleep on the board floor without rocks and sticks stabbing my ribs—only wonderful, scratchy straw that made me sneeze. I dozed until clomping footsteps filled the loft and the glow of a candle cast shadowy figures on the ceiling. The voices were my family.

"Everyone hurry and get settled," Momma whispered. "We're back on the trail in the morning."

Nancy moaned. "But I'm not sleepy."

"Story." Charlie sounded defiant.

Papa whispered, "We're too tired for stories. Hush now. Lie still so you don't disturb the Muellers."

I listened to breathing patterns for an hour or more. When the last wiggles and squirms ceased, I sat up, allowing the straw pallet to crinkle on purpose. No one stirred. I tiptoed across the creaky floor and down the stairs in the quiet darkness.

A half-moon gave just enough light to see the container. I eased it from the shelf and turned to place it on the table. Someone was sitting in a chair. I clasped my hand over my mouth to keep from screaming.

"That you, Mary?" The shadowy figure whispered. "It's me, Hans. I couldn't sleep."

"Land sakes. You scared me." I felt for my apron and sighed. *It's upstairs.*

Hans stood. "Is something wrong?"

"I need to treat my sore foot, but left my bandages upstairs."

He brushed past me and opened a drawer. "There are some here. Sit down. I'll help you."

"No. You'll get me in trouble. Please go away."

He eased a chair out for me. "Is that why you ignored me this evening?"

"Yes. My parents won't approve." I sat on the chair and pulled my heel into the seat, feeling where to put the salve.

"Here." Hans handed bandages to me, but didn't leave.

I wrapped my foot, then gazed at his silhouette in front of me. "Thank you for your help. I didn't want Momma to know about the wound."

"You're silly to keep it from her. Why not tell her?"

"She has enough to worry about." As I stood, something in the salve made the ball of my foot tingle, turn warm, and then go numb.

Hans slid the container back onto the shelf and stepped in front of me. He raised my right hand to his lips and kissed it. I ignored the impulse to pull my hand away. *What am I doing?* His body moved closer. The drum in my chest beat "to arms," but I didn't step back. He eased closer with puckered lips. I closed my eyes, pursed my lips, and tilted my head back, ready for my first kiss—it landed on my forehead.

My gut seized as if he'd punched me. My eyes popped open and watered.

Still holding my hand, he shook his head. "I...can't give you a real kiss. I may never see you again. Fredrick and I might join the Continentals. Perhaps war will be avoided or at least come to a speedy end. Then I want to come find you."

"Please don't." My eyes burned. I moved toward the stairs without looking up. "Thank you for your help."

"You're hurt, and I'm truly sorry. I would kiss you now, but your first kiss should come from the man you love. Then you'll be glad I didn't steal it. Good night." He kissed my hand, released it, and stepped away with a sigh.

The floorboards creaked behind me, and a door closed.

"Good night." I crept up the stairs, refusing to cry.

Chapter Eight

August 26

Wafts of fried bacon and coffee triggered images of Jinks and Toloman and woke me with a racing heart. A quick glance around the loft at my family calmed me. I took a few deep breaths and shook my head. The memory of Hans kissing my forehead instead of my lips brought a smile. *How silly of me to get upset.*

"Up and at 'em." Papa stooped and rolled his bedding. "I smell breakfast."

Momma nodded. "Bless the Muellers."

I sat up and slipped my moccasins on under the covers so no one would see the bandages on my foot. After gathering my bedding, I followed my family downstairs, anticipating Hans's smile in greeting.

"*Guten morgen.*" Mr. and Mrs. Mueller greeted us, but Hans and Fredrick weren't in the room.

Mrs. Mueller placed a bowl of steamy oatmeal in the center of the table before sitting. "Please excuse Hans and Fredrick. They went for early hunt but bid all goodbye and safe travels."

Chattering ensued around the table, but I tuned them out. *Cowards! Escaping into the woods rather than facing Katie and me with proper goodbyes.* I huffed too loud.

Momma frowned at me.

"Something is wrong?" Mrs. Mueller tilted her head.

Everyone stared at me, waiting. I swallowed, then smiled. "I'm sorry. It's just that I've enjoyed your wonderful home and hospitality so much I hate to leave." *Not a complete lie.*

Mrs. Mueller beamed. "I'm pleased for you to enjoy."

Momma narrowed her eyes at me before glancing away with a head shake.

The buttery, honey-sweetened oats warmed my chest and soothed my hurt feelings.

Momma and Papa nodded at each other. He stood first. "Thank you again for your hospitality. We need to be on our way now."

"You have been a great blessing." Momma rose with her empty plate and gave me and Katie a dubious glance. "Can you two manage to gather fresh plantain and hurry back while I help Mrs. Mueller with the dishes?"

We pushed our chairs back and answered, "Yes, ma'am," at the same time.

After retrieving the baskets and descending the stone steps, Katie lifted the corner of her petticoat and grinned. "Race you." She darted toward the creek, and I waved her on, not wanting to aggravate the sore on my foot, which seemed much better.

When I arrived at the bank, Katie wiggled her head, glaring. "What's your problem?"

Before I could answer, she dipped her basket into the creek, raised it dripping wet, and tossed what hadn't leaked out into my face before I could turn my head. I coughed and sputtered as she went for a refill.

I rushed behind her and shoved. She landed belly-first in the creek, and I cringed with immediate remorse. "I'm sorry."

Katie staggered up the bank, laughing and wringing out her petticoat. "You're too serious. I'm glad Fredrick wasn't here this morning. I would have been embarrassed. Momma gave me a stern talking-to yesterday. But I enjoyed being kissed. I must be like Olivia. Did Hans kiss you too?"

Irritation returned. "No, and I don't want to talk about it. Momma said to hurry. Now, look at us. We have to explain why we're soaked."

Katie frowned and picked leaves. In a moment, she held her stomach, laughing again. "Poor Mrs. Mueller will have a conniption, wondering what happened."

I imagined the scene but didn't smile. "I'm more worried about Momma. Let's hurry."

Papa, George, and Mr. Mueller had the horses loaded when Katie and I rushed into the yard out of breath.

"Sorry it took so long." I didn't explain.

Mrs. Mueller gasped.

"Land sakes." Momma shook her head.

Our siblings snickered, but Charlie frowned. "Swim."

Papa grinned and wiped sweat from his brow.

Momma motioned us inside and turned with a scowl. "You can forget about Hans and Fredrick as future husbands. Imagine what the Muellers must think of you two."

I pressed my lips together to keep from grinning.

Mrs. Mueller entered the cabin a moment later and pulled a small wooden box from the cabinet. "Please take this tea. It will help calm the girls."

"No. Please don't waste your valuable tea, Matilda. These girls are only suffering from infatuations."

Mrs. Mueller's hand rose to her mouth as she chuckled. "*Ach,* I see."

There had been no shipments of tea for two years because of the protest in Boston, but Mrs. Mueller was willing to share with us. My face flushed. "I'm sorry we worried you."

Mrs. Mueller smiled and took Katie's and my wet hands. "Maybe we can have tea in the future." She winked. "Now, go to Kentucky. I'll finish the dishes."

Papa peeked inside. "Ready?"

Momma nodded. She wrapped the plantain leaves in a clean cloth and lay her hand on Mrs. Mueller's arm. "It's been a pleasure to meet you and share your home."

Mrs. Mueller smiled. "We were pleased to meet your sweet family."

I glanced around the cheerful cabin. *I'll have a nice home like this someday.* "Please tell Hans I said goodbye."

Mrs. Mueller nodded with a beaming grin. "*Ja.* I tell him."

Drummer trotted beside Papa's horse as we strolled back to the westerly trail. I hoped Hans would emerge and say goodbye himself, but there were no shuffling sounds in the woods from any direction.

When Papa held his hand up for us to stop, my heart leapt. I strained my neck to see around Little Sis. Instead of Hans, a magnificent doe grazed on a patch of dandelions in the clearing. She glanced up.

Papa reached for his rifle, but then lowered his arm. His movement spooked the doe into the brush. He shook his head. "I forgot we have to be quiet now. We're on an old part of the Cherokee's hunting trail they've been using to—"

Momma cleared her throat, and Papa hushed.

My gut knotted, remembering Mr. Mueller's mention of the raid a month ago.

He nodded to Momma's wide eyes. "I'm not expecting trouble—just want to stay on the cautious side. We should reach the blockhouse at the Wittens' place by midafternoon. I hear they turn out a tasty cider from wild crab apples." He licked his lips and stepped away in a brisk pace.

One by one, we inched ahead. A few moments later, a crackle of rifle fire rang out from the Muellers' meadow behind us.

I sucked in a gnat and coughed. *Hans and Fredrick were nearby. They shot the doe for their supper. Cowards. I never want to see Hans again.* Momma's "guard your heart" made sense now. If Katie and I hadn't been so secluded all our lives, maybe we'd have more sense. *I must ignore the luring smiles of handsome young men from here on out.*

But within a few steps, the memory of water trickling down Han's neck awakened the tingling sensations. I snickered. Charlie glanced back at me with his finger to his lips. I clasped my mouth and chuckled.

The only sounds we contributed to the woodlands were the shuffling of leaves under our feet and an occasional snort from one of the horses clearing its nostrils. Each hour Papa stood still and listened, then he and George searched the ground, shrubs, and trees for recent human activity. I held my breath and listened for twigs breaking or anything large shuffling through the leaves. *Why did I have to eavesdrop on Papa and Mr. Mueller?* In one place, shrieking blue jays startled me so much I almost shouted, "hush." As we moved away from them, the sweeter songs of wrens and sparrows soothed my frayed nerves.

At the fourth hour, Papa lingered longer, examining a large birch tree. I stepped beside him. "What is it?" *It's worse not knowing.*

He finished scanning the tree before him. "Recent messages. The Indians leave one another carvings and paintings."

Before I could ask what about, Papa raised his finger to his lips and went to another location. I stepped in front of the tree. The outer bark had been trimmed away, and human stick figures were carved into the soft inner bark. Some held bows with arrows, some tomahawks in one hand while holding up strands of something in the other. My breath caught at the sight of other figures lying diagonally, as if on the ground. *The raid?* I stumbled back.

George eased up beside me. "Papa said some Cherokee, led by a man dragging a canoe, are bragging about a recent raid and how many settlers they scalped."

Papa pointed at George. He hushed.

Bile rose in my throat. I held my hand over my mouth as tears filled my eyes. I went to Momma, plopped down beside her, and buried my face on her shoulder, sucking in deep breaths to keep from heaving. Momma put her free arm around me and held her belly with the other.

"I'm scared," I whispered.

She rested her head on mine and spoke in a soothing tone. "Yea, though I walk through the valley of the shadow of death..."

"...I will fear no evil." I completed that portion of the Bible verse and sighed. Fear remained nonetheless, and tears wet my cheeks.

Papa approached, holding his arm out to Momma. She took it, and he helped her stand.

"Two more hours." He sounded cheerful as he smiled at her.

I stuffed plantain leaves in my shoe before standing and shook my petticoat with extra vigor, cooling my legs and trying to rid myself of the doubt that had crept in. *Where was divine protection for those settlers? Why are we testing God?*

Chapter Nine

Papa reached the top of the ridge and turned his head toward us, beaming. "We've made it. And what a spectacular sight. Come see all the crabapple trees."

Momma stepped beside Papa and gasped. "Oh, it's lovely."

"Are they really apples?" George leaned over the edge.

Momma pulled George back. "No. But I hear they're good for jelly and pickles too, not just cider." She grinned at Papa.

My sisters gasped, then echoed each other. "How pretty."

I held Charlie's hand tighter, then stepped into the clearing and moved to the cliff edge. My breath caught. Below the feathery clouds of sunset rose, orange, and gold were the rolling sage-green hills that surrounded a valley of shimmering crimson and amber treetops.

Charlie pulled my hand. "No. Scared."

I knelt and wrapped my arm around his waist. "It's all right. We won't fall."

"Looks like the trail meanders in an easy walk. Follow me." Papa led us down a winding, grassy trail.

The path soon straightened into a powdery wagon road and led through an orchard of grape-sized apples dangling above our heads in shades of yellowish red.

A picketed wall emerged on the other side. The south-facing gates were propped opened to the comings and goings of only a few scruffy-looking men with pack mules. *Why are the gates wide open?*

Papa held up his hand. "Wait in the shade of those trees." He pointed to a few scraggly oaks at the secluded western end of the fort and handed his horse's lead to George. I lingered behind and watched. Papa stepped up to a young soldier at the gate, who pointed to something inside. When Papa left my sight, the soldier tipped his hat to me. Embarrassed, I turned away and joined my family.

"Someone take Sally, please." Momma sat on the ground cross-legged, fanning herself with her petticoat.

I held my hand out to Sally, who refused to leave Momma's side, and plopped down in her lap. *No you don't.* I released Rebel's rope and plucked Sally up and into my arms. She tried to wiggle free. "Be still now. Momma wants to rest without you."

"Down," she moaned, pushing against my chest while kicking her legs.

I set her firmly on the ground and held her still. "I'll let you up after you calm down."

She pooched out her lip and stopped kicking. I nodded and released her to stand. "Stay with me." She glanced back at Momma, who had pulled her legs toward her chest to lay her head on her knees.

Poor Momma. She looked frail and exhausted. *I hope she can have a straw pallet tonight.*

"I'm sorry, dear." Papa rushed back to help her stand. "We'll set up camp out here and let the men have the fort."

I glanced at Momma for signs of worry, then back to Papa. "Shouldn't we be inside the fort for protection?"

Papa shook his head. "No. We're safer out here."

How can we be safe so far from the enclosure? What about the Cherokee?

My nerves unraveled as I helped George unload the tents. Papa had been pensive all day, watching for Cherokee. *Why are we safer here than inside the fort?* "I'll be back."

I left George, Katie, and Lizzy erecting the larger tent and went to Papa at the fire pit.

"I don't understand. Why aren't we staying inside? What about the tree paintings? Are we out of danger?"

He added more sticks to the fire. "Scouts are on patrol all around us. If there's trouble, we'll go inside."

George arrived to help Charlie roll a larger log up to Papa. I waited until they raced away before mustering a respectful tone. "I mean no disrespect, Papa, but I remember your story about the scouts at Camp Pleasant missing the signs of Chief Cornstalk's warriors the night before the battle at the Point. What if we're attacked while we sleep?"

Papa cleared his throat. "This is a different situation." His voice contained a slight edge as he turned toward Momma. "Fire's ready."

Momma glanced between us as she arrived, but said nothing.

Why won't he tell me what's wrong? I followed Papa to the edge of our camp. He stared at the fort, and I eased beside him, remaining quiet.

He sighed. "I can't guarantee anything. But the encampment is cramped, filthy, and filled with crude men. You and your sisters are safer out here in the open." He turned to me with raised eyebrows. "It's time to trust me again." His tone was serious, but not angry.

"Yes, sir." I glanced at Drummer, who lay beside a tree with his head resting on a paw. He peered at me with sad eyes. "May I please give Drummer some attention?"

Papa nodded and walked toward the horses.

Drummer's body wagged all over as I squatted and scratched him behind the ears. "Good boy." I untied his rope. "Want to go for a walk?" *At least I can peek inside as we pass the fort.*

As we neared the gate, I ignored hat-tipping and under-the-breath whistles from passing men. The view was blocked. I glanced back toward our camp. No Papa in sight. *Just a fast peek.* I crossed the threshold, sidestepped to the left, and stood still against the wall—breathing heavy. Once my heart slowed back down, I scanned the small enclosure.

One large blockhouse loomed in the center of the yard. A few lean-to-style cabins flanked the north wall. Out of place—a lone canvas tent in the back west corner and a woman wearing an ankle-length buckskin dress and moccasins. Yellow strips of cloth wove through her long black hair. She immersed a linen chemise into a steaming laundry kettle; stirred and poked the garment a few times with a stick, then pulled it out—the most brilliant red I'd ever seen.

Maybe she'll tell me how to make that red dye. I tugged on Drummer's rope. My heart raced as we eased along the wall toward the woman. Drummer sniffed the air and bristled, but didn't growl.

The woman faced the clothesline, humming a tune I didn't recognize as she hung the chemise.

I cleared my throat. "Sorry to bother you, ma'am."

She jumped and jerked her tanned face my direction. Fierce brown eyes glared as she spoke.

"Watcha doin' here? No place for baby girls."

Her lack of manners and gravelly voice unnerved me. *Run.* I took a deep breath—*No.* I greeted her with a polite curtsy. "I'm here with my family. We're moving to Kentucky territory." I pointed to her kettle. "I'd like to know how you made that beautiful red dye." *Please hurry before I get caught.*

The woman's manner softened, and she grinned with rotting teeth. "Caintuck?" Her breath reeked. "My mother's people—Shawnee." Her mouth turned down as her eyes watered. "White man—father." She spat on the ground before peering at me. "Sold me to white trapper when young like you. Man died. Now, I have many men. You have a man?"

"No." I gulped with the realization of what she asked. Sweat dribbled down my temples.

"Good." She stepped to the kettle. "Shawnee dye—secret. You keep secret?"

"Yes, ma'am." I half-smiled, still reeling.

She stared deep into my eyes, but I didn't flinch.

The woman nodded. "I show you." She motioned with a gnarled finger. "Come."

I glanced toward the gate, swallowed the lump in my throat, and tied Drummer to the tree before stepping inside. *I'll stay at the entrance.* A wooden frame held a straw-stuffed bed covered with wool blankets. She knelt in front of it and patted. "Sit."

I shook my head and gulped. "I'm sorry, ma'am. I can't stay long."

She shrugged and reached under the bed. "My Shawnee name mean leaf whispering in the wind—Whispering Leaf, but men call me Whore Woman."

My stomach churned at her words.

She dragged out a wooden box and opened it, then looked at me. "What is name?"

"Mary." Panic gripped my chest. "I'm sorry, ma'am. But I must hurry."

She approached and handed me a piece of birch wood with a detailed painting of what looked like a plant called Lady's Bedstraw. "You know this plant?"

I nodded.

She stepped to a clump of twisted roots hanging from the top of the tent, broke off a piece, and placed it in my palm while holding onto my hand. "Simmer root in tin pot overnight. Add pee to set color. Understand?"

"Yes, ma'am, thank you." I smiled.

She caressed the back of my hand and smiled into my eyes. "Soft."

A shiver ran up my spine. I stepped back and slipped the root into my apron pocket.

She let go and nodded. "You make good life in Caintuck. Make many babies. Remember Whispering Leaf."

"Mary?" Papa's voice sounded close and panicked.

I rushed from the tent out of breath. "I'm here, Papa."

He stood at the tree with Drummer, staring at me with glazed eyes. His face seemed pale.

"I'm sorry, Papa. I took Drummer for a walk, saw this woman making a red dye, and—"

"No excuse." His nostrils flared. He pointed toward the gate and led the way at a fast pace.

My legs wobbled as I caught up to him. He stopped and turned to me. "Do you know what that woman is?"

His glare made my eyes water. "Yes, sir." I sniffled. "She told me what the men call her." Tears fell—not from Papa's rebuke, but from knowing Whisper's horrible life.

Papa shook his head. "Do you understand the danger of this place for our family?"

"Yes, sir." I wiped tears from my eyes.

He stormed away and tied Drummer to the lead line with the horses.

Momma raised her eyebrows at me and took a deep breath. "Be thankful we care enough to be angry with you." She raked coals to the side of the fire.

I sat on the ground with my knees pulled to my chest, weeping from Momma's chastisement and the guilt of sneaking into the fort without permission.

A small hand patted my back. I peeked out. Sally stood beside me. I sniffed and took her into my arms for a hug. "Thank you for helping me feel better."

Katie and Lizzy were playing tag with Charlie and the younger girls, but glanced my way from time to time. I stood, ready to receive additional correction from Momma so I could show her the root.

"The woman in the fort makes a beautiful red dye with this root." I held it out to her.

She scratched it with her fingernail and nodded. "Lady's Bedstraw. We can try it out once we are settled. Is that why you disregarded your papa's warning to stay out of the fort?"

I looked at the ground. "Yes, ma'am. I'm sorry."

"Well, lesson learned then." She stood from the fire pit, then crumpled into a heap on the ground.

"Momma!" I knelt and rolled her over, brushing the dirt from her cheek.

Papa rushed back from the horses. "Katherine?"

She opened her eyes and sucked in a deep breath, chuckling. "I stood too fast."

Papa helped her stand.

I took her hand. "I can take over supper while you rest."

"No. No. I'm all right now. Get the book. We need story time while these rabbits cook. I want to know what became of poor Olivia."

I didn't feel like reading, but I retrieved the book and shouted for my siblings. "Momma wants story time." I sighed and dropped the root into a waterproof pouch in my saddlebag.

Katie and Lizzy corralled Charlie and Nancy and followed me to the fire pit.

"I have to go in the bushes first." Susie waved.

George snapped a stick for kindling and moaned. "Do I have to come?"

Papa shook his head. "I'll take George and Charlie with me. I want to verify the route for tomorrow."

"Not long." Momma sat. "Dinner will be ready in a few short minutes."

"Yes, ma'am." Papa tipped his hat. George and Charlie beamed.

After Susie sat down, we read.

When Papa and George returned a few minutes later, Papa handed Momma a small crock. "Pickled crab apples."

"Oh." Momma squealed. "What a wonderful surprise."

"Should I stop reading?" I hoped. The story had become like a torturous punishment for Katie's and my recent escapade with the Mueller twins. Even Katie squirmed a few times as I read.

Momma shook her head. "Finish the chapter. We're in suspense."

I concluded chapter twenty-one with the shocking account of Olivia's demise upon running away to marry the wretched Squire Thornhill, then fleeing from his villainous attempt to force her into prostitution.

Poor Whispering Leaf. My heart broke for the fort woman forced into prostitution by her own papa. She's lonely for softness in her life. *That's why she caressed my hand.* I sighed. *Why does she stay? Why can't she return to the Shawnee?*

"I knew that squire was no good." Katie bumped my arm. "Poor Olivia."

Papa's good humor returned. "Let her story be a lesson to you. Not everyone who elopes ends up happy, like Momma and me."

"Michael. Hush." Momma held her flushed face.

I chuckled.

"You and Momma eloped?" Lizzy smiled, hearing the news for the first time.

"That's a story for another time. Let's eat." Momma changed the subject. She had said those same words to me when I asked about their courtship years ago.

Papa laughed and winked. "Bow heads."

After a few bites, Papa belched and leaned back. "Sixteen miles to our next campsite. Then the next day, we should be at Elk Garden. We'll buy grain at the mill and restock our jerky. I sent a letter to Daniel Boone when we arrived at Wood's Fort, asking him to wait another week so we can join his party. I asked him to leave a reply at Elk Garden."

He hadn't mentioned the letter before. The knowledge filled me with hope. Traveling with a group would relieve my worries of being pursued by Tories and watched for by Cherokee. A wave of fear fluttered in my chest. "But what if he decides not to wait? Will we wait for others, like Mr. Mueller suggested?"

Papa narrowed his eyes. "There won't be others until October. We'll continue to Kentucky." He sounded annoyed.

"I didn't mean to sound testy, Papa. I just wanted to know if you'd changed your mind. I'm worried is all."

Momma pointed at me. "You're hoping Hans will come for you." Her curt voice stunned me.

Papa frowned and cocked his head toward her. She didn't flinch.

"No, Momma." I took a deep breath. "I promise...I'm over Hans." My eyes watered. "I'm...afraid of Indian attacks."

Momma's face softened. "I didn't mean to be harsh. I'm sorry, dear. I don't know what is wrong with me this afternoon. I need to go lie down." She stood, steadied herself, and then held her arms out to me.

I cuddled in her arms. "I understand why you asked, though."

Papa shifted on the stump where he sat. "Something I need to know about?"

I shook my head and took a bite of the tart crab apple pickle that made my mouth pucker and my teeth hurt.

He shook his head at me. "Are you ever going to trust me?"

The look of hurt in his eyes broke my heart. *How do I explain myself to him when I don't understand myself?*

Chapter Ten

August 28

For two days, the terrain remained mostly level, which allowed my foot to heal, but the scenery became monotonous. It was late in the afternoon of our sixth day from Indian Creek when the pickets of Elk Garden Fort freed me from a mental fog. We entered the gate and dismounted. This fort, like Wittens', had one large blockhouse in the center of the yard but many cabins.

A man wearing a dark-blue hunting shirt with a red waist sash greeted Papa with a smile and a friendly handshake. There was a strip of red cloth sewn onto his right shoulder.

"Welcome, Mr. Shirley, and ma'am." He tipped his hat to Momma. "I'm sorry to inform you that Captain Boone's party insisted on departing on the twenty-fifth. He's leaving a map for you at Moore's Fort. You're two days out, but you're welcome to wait for the

Hendersons. I don't likely know when to expect them. Judge Henderson had to face opposition in North Carolina and Virginia about the legality of his treaty."

"Thank you, Sergeant Kincaid." Papa shook his hand again. "We'll just stay the night."

The sergeant pointed to the front west corner. "Set your tent up there. Let me know if you need anything." He tipped his hat again to Momma and stepped away with Papa.

Opposition? I wanted to eavesdrop further, but Momma motioned me away. "Did Papa know there was opposition? What will happen to claims if settlement rights are denied?"

Momma sighed. "I don't know. Please, take Charlie and Nancy to the privy." She pointed toward a white stone privy just outside the gate.

"Yes, ma'am." I took Charlie's hand and motioned for Nancy to follow.

Upon opening the weathered privy door, I gagged. Fresh diarrhea on the bench seat ran down the front onto the floor. "This is too horrible. Come with me."

I led Charlie and Nancy to the bushes a few feet away. "Go in here. No one will bother you." I stood guard while they maneuvered out of sight.

In a few minutes, Charlie shouted. "Need leaves."

"Me too," Nancy said. "The ones in here are too small."

Glancing around at the nearby trees, I spotted a hickory with large green leaves. "I'll be back."

I gathered two handfuls and returned to see an elderly man aiming his rifle toward the bushes. I rushed to him shouting, "No. There are children in there."

The man lowered his rifle and scowled at me. "What in the tarnation they doin' in there? I thought they be rabbits."

He reeked of whiskey and stale urine. I stepped upwind and glared into his glassy eyes. "The privy is too filthy."

He flinched. "Dad-blame-it, girly. Ya got eyes like a wildcat. Get back inside the gate 'fore ya be scalped or carried off." The man staggered away, but his stench lingered. I passed leaves to Charlie and Nancy until they emerged from cover.

Nancy's eyes were wide. "He was about to shoot us."

"Don't say anything to Momma about it. I'll tell her." I took their hands and hurried back inside.

Momma was untying a food packet as we approached.

"Can't use that privy. It's worse than nasty. The bushes aren't safe either." I waited for Momma to look at me. "A drunken old man almost shot Charlie and Nancy because he thought they were rabbits."

"Land sakes. Guess I'll have to wait until our tent is up and we can use a chamber pot."

"Me too." I turned around to go help with the tents, but men were there with Papa and George.

They raised the big tent with tall poles to accommodate all of us, like a small cabin. Some of the men rolled stumps to a fire pit, and others made a small table from rough planks. I smiled. *Men of character.* Curiosity struck. *Does this mean Papa has decided to stay?*

I went to Rebel, untied my bedroll, and stood with Katie and Lizzy.

"It's ready." George waved.

Susie carried an armload of blankets inside before us. "Are we all going to sleep in here?"

The tent was too small for anything on the dirt floor but our pallets.

"Yes." Momma chuckled. "The first thing we're going to do is set up a privacy corner."

I laid my pallet down. "Are we going to stay for a while, like the sergeant suggested?"

"No. Papa and I agreed to go on to Fort Boonesborough—no reason to stay. I want to get there and be settled again. Help me secure a blanket in this corner so we can relieve ourselves without catching our deaths."

Once we all took turns in the corner, I volunteered to go empty it.

I carried the chamber pot to a cleaner-looking privy behind a large cabin in the back corner, stepped inside, and poured out the contents.

"You sure that's the traitor Cage, with his family?" A man's voice boomed.

My heart raced as I eased the squeaky door closed and latched it.

"'Twas Toloman said so." Another man spoke.

I gasped.

"I know that's his dad-blamed daughter over thar. She had me and Jinks—God rest his useless soul—downright bamboozled, dressed like a boy. But while we chawed, she gave up her pa's name and his 'filiation with that no-'count McWar."

It's…Toloman. My stomach churned.

"We can claim the bounty if we kill 'em," the second voice said. "And after we're done with the girl, we can trade her off to the Injuns."

Someone pulled at the door. "Tarnation. Who's in thar takin' so long?" A fourth, deeper voice spoke.

I pretended to throw up.

"Well…you jest keep this'n then."

"Let's move 'way from here," Toloman said.

When the shuffling of leaves stopped, I eased the door open and went in the direction I'd heard the voices. *I need to see the other men so I can tell Papa.* I stepped behind a large oak tree and peeked around. My blood ran cold.

There he is.

The four men stood together, pointing toward our tent and frowning as they spoke among themselves. My feet wouldn't move. *Breathe. Move away. Must tell Papa.*

Pushing away from the tree, I sucked in a deep breath, retreated back toward the privy, and ran to Papa, who was talking to a few men near our horses.

"Papa!"

He turned to me as I dropped the bucket and fell into his arms. I didn't care who saw. "Toloman...the man who shoved me from my horse." I took a deep breath. "Plotting against us. The four men in the back corner to your left." I pointed.

Papa moved his head slightly. "I see them. Go to Momma, but don't tell her. I'll get word to the sergeant." He pulled me back and looked into my eyes. "You're trembling. Can you walk?"

I nodded and retrieved the bucket. When I lumbered inside the tent out of breath, Momma glanced up. "What's wrong?"

"Privy made me queasy. I need to lie down." I placed our chamber bucket behind the privacy blanket and returned to lie on my pallet. *What's going to happen now?*

In a few minutes, Papa stepped inside, frowning. He squatted in front of me, searching my eyes. "Sorry, polliwog. I have to take you to the blockhouse to give testimony."

I clutched my throat and struggled to breathe.

Momma rushed to me. "What's wrong?"

Papa whispered in her ear. She gasped and stepped back.

He helped me sit up and stand.

"I might have to throw up." I swallowed bile.

Momma handed me a cloth and stroked my hair. "Carry this with you in case."

I peered at Papa. "Must I face those men?" My voice quavered.

Papa's lips pressed into a straight line as he stepped beside me and held out his arm. "Yes. But they can't hurt you. I'll stand nearby. Just tell the sergeant what you heard and point out the man you know as Toloman."

As Papa and I left the tent, several men stopped to stare. My heart pounded, and my knees buckled, but Papa held me upright until I could stand on my own. My stomach churned. I fought for each breath as we arrived at the blockhouse and stepped inside. A stifling room full of voices fell silent. For a moment, everything went dark.

Papa sat me in a chair and peered into my eyes. "Mary. Breathe."

I focused on his face as he stepped back. Sudden movement in front of me forced my gaze from the comfort of Papa to the shuffling crowd. Four men stepped forward and stood side by side.

The sergeant moved beside me and cleared his throat. "Miss Shirley, can you please tell us if these are the men you're accusing of conspiring against your father and involved in treasonous activity?"

I took a deep breath and scanned each one. Anger replaced fear when Toloman smirked.

Emboldened, I stood and cleared my throat. "These are the men I overheard from the privy, desiring to kill my papa and sell me to the Indians. When they left the privy area, I followed so I could see them together and confirm the identity of that man." I pointed. "Toloman. I met him two weeks ago"—I glanced at Papa—"but I can't say how. He's associated with Patriot enemies."

Murmurs erupted in the room.

For a brief moment, my mind replayed every vivid detail of being shoved from my horse, kicked in the ribs, and almost raped. Without thinking, I worked up a mouthful of spit, stepped in front of Toloman, and spewed spit in his face. Laughter broke out from the observers in the blockhouse. I felt ashamed but justified.

"That will be all, Miss Shirley. You may go now. Thank you." The sergeant smiled.

I couldn't move. Papa took my arm and led me away, whispering, "Are you all right?"

"No. Having to be the center of attention was horrible." My body quaked. I stopped and looked at him. "What will happen now?"

Papa's face became serious. "They'll be kept under guard until the sergeant decides their sentences. Rest assured; they'll never be allowed to harm us. I'll explain everything to the family. You don't have to talk about it anymore. You made me proud." He pulled me into his arms, and I rested my head on his chest—comforted.

We continued to the fire pit, where Momma stood staring at me, wringing her hands.

She rushed to wrap her arms around me, then pulled back to peer into my eyes.

I smiled and took a deep breath. "I'm all right."

"Sit and rest. We have everything about ready for supper." She removed the lid from the cast-iron pot and stirred what smelled like squirrel stew. Papa went to check on the horses.

In a few minutes, he came back with George and a map. They sat opposite me and talked about how to calculate distance based on terrain.

Katie and Susie were making hoecakes but glanced at me from time to time to smile. We hadn't had hoecakes since we left home. I smiled back. Nancy was teaching Charlie to recite his twos in arithmetic. "Where are Lizzy and Sally?" I asked.

"Sally was bored and fussy, so Lizzy took her for a walk." Momma placed the lid on the pot and stood.

A few minutes later, Lizzy rushed toward Momma, pulling a bawling Sally by the hand. Sally threw herself down, protesting. "More walk."

"Hush now. Go to Mary." Momma lifted Sally to her feet and went to Lizzy. "What is it?"

Sally hushed but pooched out her lip and sat on the ground beside me, with her arms and legs crossed.

Lizzy's eyes were big as she panted. "Something terrible. I can't say out loud." She took a deep breath.

Papa rolled the map as he ushered her and Momma past me and into the tent, but didn't lower the flap. I wasn't close enough to read their lips, but Momma raised a hand to her mouth. Papa hugged Lizzy. Momma stayed inside with Lizzy as Papa stepped out and headed to the blockhouse at a fast pace.

What now? I shook my head and my eyes watered.

I took Sally by the hand and began a game of chase with her, Nancy, and Charlie. When Lizzy and Momma came out of the tent, I poured water from the canteen into a cup and sat beside Lizzy. "I brought you a cup of water."

Lizzy sniffled and took the cup. "Thank you."

I leaned back on my hands, stretched my legs out with ankles crossed, and waited. Lizzy finished drinking and sighed. She leaned to my ear. "Two men lying together in the bushes like a rooster on a hen."

I gasped and hugged Lizzy. *Another disturbing image.*

"I'm all right now, but I don't want to talk about it." Lizzy handed me the cup, and I stood.

As I stepped away from her, Katie and Susie watched me with piercing eyes. George pretended to play with

Charlie but eased closer. I addressed them all. "I can't tell you what Lizzy saw."

Momma turned to us. "Papa is taking care of things, and after supper, we'll have a talk."

Papa removed his hat as he approached and gave Momma a kiss before sitting.

Momma sighed. "We need to talk to our children after we eat about the realities of life on the frontier."

"How much do we have to tell them?" Papa frowned.

Momma sighed. "Everything. It's best to hear about life from us."

Papa nodded. "Let's eat first—I need to think on it."

We all had knowledge of begetting from observing our farm animals, but I didn't understand this act.

We ate outside around the table with a warm breeze circulating through our petticoats. My youngest siblings talked about their day of play, but the rest of us were quiet. I struggled not to cry over the traumas of the day but longed to go back to the Muellers, where we had been comfortable and happy.

"Clean up and repack the plates and utensils while I talk to Momma a minute." Papa led her into the tent.

"What did you see?" George whispered to Lizzy.

I glared at him. "Leave her alone. You'll find out soon enough if Papa wants you to know."

Lizzy ignored stares as she dried her plate and fork. I could tell she was still troubled because she was silent instead of chattering.

Papa and Momma returned. Momma sat with her hands folded and a serious expression. Papa took a deep breath as everyone sat. Charlie climbed into my lap out of habit, and I instinctively rocked him from side to side.

Papa cleared his throat. "Lizzy saw two men in the bushes pleasuring each other."

"You mean kissing and hugging?" George tilted his head.

"Yes," Momma answered before Papa or Lizzy explained further.

Katie winced. "Why?"

"Because their passion for each other led them to. This has taken place as long as men and women have lived on the earth. There will be many things people do that we disagree with, but people have to choose for themselves. Even those who believe the way we do can't follow the Bible teachings perfectly. We don't understand everything, and therefore we leave it to God." He sighed and scanned our faces.

"Momma and I are responsible for ourselves and our children. Someday you must decide to follow the way we teach or decide a different way for your family. This is what freedom of religion is about. Your grandparents fled the Rhineland of Germany because they wanted to follow the teachings of Martin Luther. Many people were beaten and killed by those who wanted everyone to be Catholic. Our family is neither of these, but we're allowed to choose."

"What are we?" I shook my head.

Papa laughed. "Maybe there's not a name for us." He smiled at Momma. She nodded and smiled back.

I liked Papa's answer. I liked the freedom to read the Bible and decide for myself if it's a good way or not.

"Time for sleep now." Momma directed Sally and Charlie to their pallets inside.

A volley of drumbeats erupted near the central blockhouse. We leapt up at the same time, and Papa already had his rifle in hand. "It's not 'to arms' at least but stay here." Papa walked toward the blockhouse, where the fort inhabitants were gathering. I maneuvered my head until I could see. As the drums beat, the two men Lizzy had seen were being chased out of the fort with just the clothes on their backs and their rifles.

Papa returned, and our eyes met. "But it's getting dark, and the men have no supplies. Why?" I asked.

"I have no answers. Pray for them." Papa moved forward. "Let's get back to the tent."

God, help them make it to a place of safety. Right or wrong, no one should be sent out into the darkness like that.

I lingered behind so I could cry freely about everything. I even prayed for the fate of the Tories.

Chapter Eleven

August 29

A gaging cough from the privacy corner concerned me. I sat up, glancing at the stirring bodies of my brothers and sisters, then discovered my parents weren't on their pallets.

The tent flap rose, and Papa stepped inside with a wet bucket. He was out of breath as he whispered, "Momma's sick." Water sloshed onto the ground as he stepped behind the blanket.

Momma hadn't been sick in several weeks. *Why now?*

I rolled my bedding to the side and discovered Sally sitting alone with her lips pooched. When I sat beside her, she lay her head in my lap. I stoked her hair and whispered, "Momma will be all right." *God, please let Momma be all right.*

The others rose for the day's travel, but I wasn't so sure we'd be leaving. Charlie scampered to where I was still sitting. "Breakfast?"

Momma emerged from behind the curtain with Papa. "I'll feel better in a few minutes. Everyone eat some jerky."

Papa held Momma's arm as she sat on a log stool, wiping her forehead and mouth. He stroked her hand. "We can rest today."

"No, I just need something in my stomach. It will pass."

When Sally toddled to Momma, I rose and retrieved the pouch of jerky. As I passed it around to the family, Lizzy blurted the question, "Are you going to have a baby?"

I glared at her. She, Katie, and I had suspected Momma's condition back in May when her bouts of morning sickness began. We'd agreed to let Momma break the news to the family.

"Yes." Momma sighed. "Sometime before the end of February."

"Like Mary." Nancy grinned at me.

George moaned. "Another baby? Keeping us awake all night?"

Papa chuckled. "It's good for you to be aware of this fact before you marry someday."

"Well, I'm going to build a separate cabin for my wife and babies." George bit off a hunk of jerky. Those of us who knew better burst out laughing.

Once I finished eating, I held my breath and retrieved the chamber pot to empty for Momma.

When I neared the tent entrance, Papa's gaze fixed on me as he raised the flap. "Don't go near the gate."

His ominous order echoed in my head all the way to the closest privy. *Why do I always want to do the very thing Papa tells me not to?* The mixture of sour urine and puke made me gag. I sucked in a fresh breath and held it before opening the privy door and going inside. I kept my head turned away, dumped the bucket's contents into the pit, and then rushed outside, inhaling fresh air.

My eyes wandered to the gate, where several men had gathered. I jerked my head away and quickened my pace back to our tent. *Something's wrong—that's all I need to know.*

As I approached, two men were at our horses speaking with Papa. They shook his hand, then passed me, tipping hats. Papa finished securing the tent on the back of his horse, then stepped in front of me. "I need to check in with Sergeant Kincaid before we leave. Everyone is packing and loading the horses, except Momma. She's heaving over a stump on the other side of the tent. Check on her in a bit. I'll be back."

"Yes, sir." *Poor Momma.*

I found our used dishwater, poured some into the bucket, and sloshed out the foulness before securing it by the handle to her pack on Sir. After washing my hands with what was left of a sliver of lye soap, I went to Rebel, who greeted me with a snort as I rubbed his neck. "Are you ready to get going again? I'm ready to get away from this place. I'm not enjoying these forts." I wiggled his saddle to check the tightness.

Momma rinsed her rag in the remaining dishwater and sat on the ground with a sigh. "I'll be better by noon or so. Thank you for taking care of the bucket."

I walked over, put my arms around her neck, and kissed her forehead. "I hope you feel better soon."

Papa returned, forcing a smile. "We're going to play a game of trust."

"What's a game of trust?" Susie stood, smiling.

"I'll explain in a minute." He looked at me. "I need the cloth strips."

What do bandages have to do with trust? I went to Sir, untied Momma's remedy bag, and reached in for the roll of bandages.

After handing them to Papa, he unrolled four long strips and draped them over his neck. He motioned for the younger children and stooped down, holding up one of the bandages. "These are blindfolds for our game. First, you'll mount the horses, then a cloth will cover your eyes so you can't see. You must not take it off until I say. It's very important not to peek. Understand?"

The children nodded.

He stood and glanced at the rest of us. "Everyone else is old enough to trust me when I say don't look."

The tightness in my stomach was no longer related to the stench from the chamber pot. *What could be so gruesome that he doesn't want us to see?*

"At least we get to ride the horses." I smiled at Charlie, then mounted with him and tied the blindfold around his eyes. His head tilted back and then bobbed from side to side. I placed my hands over his eyes. "If you don't peek, I'll let you hold the reins when your blindfold is off." He nodded and sat still.

Papa scanned us without smiling. "I give a stern warning: keep your eyes on the ground as you go through the gate, then rein your horse sharply to the right and focus straight ahead until we've rounded the corner. If you choose to look up before making the turn, the consequences are your own. Let's go." He clicked his tongue and eased Little Sis toward the gate.

I urged Rebel forward and fell in line behind George. My heart raced as I battled the urge to look up. *Don't do it. Why is the temptation so strong?* I counted Rebel's steps, then focused on the back of Charlie's head as the gate neared—ready to shield his eyes with my hand if he tried to peek. His chin rose slightly, but he lowered it and shook his head.

"Good boy. We can't look yet." I reined to the right and rocked forward. Rebel trotted around the corner.

"It's safe to remove the blindfolds." Papa's shouted. "We'll continue riding awhile."

I removed Charlie's blindfold and hugged him. "You did good." I handed him Rebel's reins as promised.

He rolled forward and gave the reins a shake, saying, "Get up."

Rebel ignored him and kept to a slow gait. Curiosity remained, but I didn't want any more images in my head. *I need to be blissfully ignorant for once.*

We stopped at a small creek and waited for Papa and George to report the all clear before dismounting.

"How many more days?" Nancy whined.

Papa chopped off an eight-inch section of grapevine, cut notches into it, and gave it to Nancy. "You can be the day keeper. I've cut a notch for each day we have been away from Indian Creek. How many are there now?"

Nancy studied it. "Seven."

"By the time we arrive at Fort Boonesborough, there will be twenty, more or less. Now, subtract seven from twenty and tell us how many days are left." He raised a finger to his lips as he glanced at the rest of us.

Nancy stared at the vine, whispering to herself.

I pulled a packet of bear jerky from my apron pocket and nibbled as we waited.

"Thirteen more days." She beamed and then frowned. "Huh, too many."

Papa smiled. "Good job. You'll have to remind me to notch it every day."

She nodded and ran to play with Charlie and Sally.

I sat with my back against a large oak tree and propped my legs over its large roots. *Almost a fortnight more of unbearable tribulations.*

George plopped down beside me, frowning. "They hung those men. I shouldn't have looked."

"Why did you tell me?" I stood and glared at him. "Don't you dare tell me anything more—not ever."

Sensing my family's stares, I rushed toward Rebel. *Four men are dead because of me. Why did they hang them? Why not send them to authorities back east?* Out of breath, I stuffed the rest of my jerky into the saddlebag and stroked the horse's neck. *George must be in torment.*

I gazed back. He held his knees to his chest with his head down. My eyes watered. I shook my head, trudged over to him, and sat. I put my arm around his shoulder. "I'm sorry to be harsh. I wish you hadn't looked. Now you'll have terrible images in your head like I do."

George sniffled. "I'm sorry."

Papa stood and stretched. "Time to go. We'll be walking now." He helped Momma up and headed for the horses.

George stood and offered his hand. "Thank you for sitting with me."

"You're welcome." I smiled and let him pull me to my feet with surprising strength. *Stop growing up.*

As I checked Rebel's legs, Papa approached. I stood, and he reached for my hand. "I'm sorry George told you about the men. I didn't want you to know and feel guilty. Are you all right?"

I shook my head. "Why weren't they sent to Williamsburg?"

"I'm afraid no one on this side of the Allegheny thinks that way." He frowned. "Justice is decided locally and carried out. Those men helped stir up trouble with the Cherokee against the settlements. I know you feel bad about their deaths, but they wouldn't have felt bad about ours nor the lives of others. Understand?"

I sighed and nodded. "There's something else troubling me."

He continued holding my hand.

"Why are we still going to Kentucky if the land deal is being opposed, like Sergeant Kincaid said? What happens to everyone's claims if it's not approved?"

His head jerked back, then shook. "You don't miss anything, do you? You might be a better spy than me." Papa leaned to my ear. "We must keep the British and their Indian allies at bay. That's part of what the dispatches you delivered were about. If the king retains control of the western settlements, the fight against tyranny will fail."

He removed his hat and wiped sweat from his forehead with his arm. "As for land claims, they'll be legitimized and filed as soon as legislators in Virginia and North Carolina stop squabbling over who has jurisdiction. The fact is, none of them liked Judge Henderson making a deal with the Cherokee independent of either colony. Judge Henderson desires his claim to be recognized as its own colony, called Transylvania. The sooner we can mark our claim and build a cabin, we'll have a jump on the land rush once it's decided. Now, lay your worries down."

"I'll try, but when will all the warring end?"

Papa held his arms open, and I stepped into his hug. "Sorry, polliwog. The Bible says we're born full of trouble. Time to get on down the trail."

I sighed. *It also says something about everything being meaningless.*

Chapter Twelve

About midday, laughter and shouts of, "You're it," echoed from a clearing ahead. Excitement fluttered like butterflies in my stomach. We entered a yard where a large two-story log house loomed with half a dozen children, playing chase. "This is the Dunkins' place." Papa held up his hand for us to stop when a couple of wiry bulldogs raced toward us, yapping in warning. Drummer growled with bristled fur, but Papa motioned for him to sit.

The other dogs stood still and barked, until a boy called them back and shouted, "Come ahead."

The boy smiled and greeted Papa with a handshake. He seemed a bit older than Lizzy. "Welcome, sir. I'm John Dunkin Junior. My da is the sergeant at Glade Hollow garrison. Do you need me to fetch him?" His musical accent sounded Scottish.

Why does he call his papa da?

"No. But if it's acceptable, we'd like to rest and eat our lunch in the shade there." Papa pointed to the scant trees.

"My granny insists travelers be invited to our table. She always prepares extra for company. I'll send our man, Donavan, to tend your horses while you rest." He pointed to an elderly black man who was raking hay into bundles.

Papa glanced back at John. "Appreciate the invitation, but we won't impose."

"I'll send him just the same." John smiled. "Here comes Granny to invite you."

A beaming-faced woman approached, waving her hands. "Save your provisions." Her manner was high-spirited. "We have plenty of beans and potatoes already cooked. Please join us. I'm Granny Dunkin."

Momma smiled and stepped forward to shake hands. "I'm Katherine Shirley. Are you sure you have enough for all of us? We can contribute."

Granny pulled Momma into an embrace as though she were a long-lost daughter, then stepped back. "No, no, we always have plenty. Please come."

I like this family so far.

We left our horses in the care of John and followed Granny to the cabin. Papa pointed to the ground near the porch, and Drummer lay down.

A slight breeze from the opened door and windows circulated the aroma of boiled potatoes and pinto beans. On the shelf near the window cooled what looked like a blackberry cobbler. I wanted to cry. Blackberry was my favorite. People of various ages were gathered around the longest table I had ever seen. They smiled and stared.

Beginning on her left, Granny pointed. "Here is my daughter-in-law, Eleanor, and her children are Elizabeth, Peggy, Joseph, Polly, and Sarah. Please welcome the Shirley family to our table."

"Welcome," they said together, and adjusted their positions around the table to make room for all of us.

"Please sit. John Junior will be in soon."

A girl, about my age, grinned and patted the seat next to her. I smiled and sat. "What is your name again? There were too many names to stick."

She laughed. "I'm Elizabeth, named after my Granny, but please call me Beth." She spoke with the same animation as Granny. "Would you like to go with me to the creek for dishwater later?"

"If my momma allows." I grinned.

John entered the cabin and took his place at the table.

Granny said a short blessing and passed the potatoes. "We'd be pleased if you folks consider settling here with us."

"Thank you for the offer." Papa smiled. "We're going on to Fort Boonesborough."

Granny frowned. "Well then, eat hearty. You'll need your strength for the long haul."

I tuned out Beth's chattering when Momma whispered to her momma, "What remedy did you use for morning sickness?"

I hadn't noticed Mrs. Dunkin being pregnant. She grinned. "Dried peppermint leaves. I have an extra bag if you're in need."

"Yes, thank you. I will be fine once we are settled." Momma ate a small bite of beans.

Beth bumped my arm with her elbow. "Did you want cobbler?"

I nodded. "Yes, please."

Granny and Beth passed out small bowls of the tangy dessert. I took my time eating and listened to Beth speak of almost being bitten by a snake as she picked the berries.

A girl next to Lizzy tugged on Mrs. Dunkin's sleeve. "May we be excused now, please?"

Mrs. Dunkin nodded.

"My children may be excused as well, but stay close." Papa spoke with his mouth full. "Enjoy a thirty-minute visit; then we'll get back on the trail." He grinned at Momma with stained teeth until she giggled.

I savored the last bite of my crunchy cobbler, then wiped my mouth and followed Beth outside.

Beth glided down the cedar-scented trail to the creek, chattering without taking her eyes off me. "Your da must be a surveyor. Most families heading to Kentucky settlements have men that are surveyors. I don't know why a place would need so many."

Da must be their term for papa. Where have I heard it before? I shrugged. "Yes. My papa aims to acquire a good parcel ahead of the rush."

"Wish you weren't going on to Kentucky, though. It would be nice to have a friend." She dipped her bucket.

I nodded. "Maybe you'll come to Fort Boonesborough someday."

"Well, it hasn't been mentioned." She stood with a sigh. "Colonel Preston gave my da charge of the Glade Hollow garrison. I suppose I'll just have to run off with a handsome traveler someday."

My jaw dropped. *How could one be as lonely as that?*

Beth held her belly and laughed. "It was funny to see the shock on your face. My da would skin me alive if I did something like that. Besides, I'm not ready to pop out as many babies as my ma." She chuckled. "Hope you have a good life in Kentucky. Just pray for your ol' friend Beth from time to time."

I shook my head at her humor and hugged her in sympathy. "I will. I hope you meet someone proper and have a good life too."

Beth seemed touched by my concern as she responded with watery eyes, "Thank you. I suppose you'll be leaving before the dishes are washed."

"Not if my momma has a say." I grinned. "We always help."

"It's doubtful. My Granny prides herself on serving folks. Suppose we better get back."

Papa, George, and John were checking the horses with a brawny black man I assumed was Donavan. When Beth and I stepped toward the porch, the man glanced up. I smiled.

He lowered his eyes the same way Big Jim and Adam had done. I understood it was something they had been trained to do, but I didn't like it.

Beth carried the bucket inside as Momma and Granny step onto the porch.

"It's time to go," Momma called to the younger children as she said goodbye to Granny and Eleanor. Granny handed her a linen bag filled with what smelled like fresh hoecakes.

"Can't we spend the night here?" Susie frowned as she walked up with a Dunkin daughter she had been chatting with.

Momma shook her head. "We have daylight left and need to make another four hours." She turned to Granny. "I wish you'd let us help with the dishes."

"Pshaw." Granny gave a wave of dismissal and grinned. "I have plenty of hands that need washing."

The younger children frowned as we gathered at our horses.

Papa shook hands with John, then turned and stretched his hand out to Donavan. "Thank you for caring for our horses."

Donavan bowed. "My pleasure, sir." He straightened and addressed John. "Is there anything else you need, young masta?"

"No, you can return to your chores now." John didn't even look at him.

John's lack of respect irritated me. I stepped toward the elderly man. "Thank you for your help."

Donavan stopped mid-stride and turned. He tipped his hat, then continued to the barn.

"Here comes my da." John pointed out a rider galloping in from a northerly direction.

The elder Dunkin slowed, then halted in the yard before dismounting.

"Hello, Sergeant Dunkin." Papa stepped toward the man.

The sergeant shook Papa's hand. "I hope you folks aren't traveling to Kentucky."

My jaw dropped. *Is there a bad report?*

"Well, sir. That's our plan." Papa stepped back. "We'll stake out our claim and get a cabin built before winter."

The sergeant shook his head. "Well, I think you're a dang fool. You're welcome to settle right here in the most fertile limestone basin in the country. At least leave your family here and go stake your claim. There's a heap of trouble going on over that Henderson deal."

His tone of voice and manner offended me. *How dare he call Papa a fool?*

"Yes, sir. I'm aware of all that." Papa sounded gruff. "We appreciate your family's hospitality, but we're heading on down the trail. I want to make Moore's Fort by tomorrow afternoon."

Sergeant Dunkin tilted up his chin. "Well then, pay close attention to the turkey calls when you cross the Cumberland. The Shawnee are staying allied with the British. You'll be all right to Moore's Fort tomorrow and probably to Blackmore's a day from there. Martin's Fort is a three-day stretch—if you don't get yourselves scalped by Cherokee. From there, it's the Almighty's mercy through the gap and beyond."

Heat swooped through my body. Sweat dribbled into my ringing ears, and I had to take deep breaths to prevent my knees from buckling.

"Thank you for the provisions and the advice, sir." Papa's eyes were narrow and his tone curt.

Sergeant Dunkin shook his head. "Good luck to ya then." He tipped his hat and strolled toward the cabin.

I didn't know who I was the most irritated with—Sergeant Dunkin for his bluntness or Papa for sounding arrogant. *Why is he ignoring the advice to wait? Now every blasted turkey gobble is going to make me ill.*

Once we were away from the Dunkins' place, Papa sang the frog courting song and Charlie bounced in time as he sang along. Perhaps it was Sergeant Dunkin's pronouncement of "You'll be fine to Moore's Fort" that lightened Papa's mood, or maybe he wanted the song stuck in our heads to drive the sergeant's words of warning away. It did calm me, and once the singing ended, I hummed every song I could remember.

Chapter Thirteen

August 30

A quarter mile from Moore's Fort, peppy high-pitched fiddle music filled the woods, and my heart fluttered. Before we neared the gate of the massive stockade, Papa tied the rope to Drummer's collar. "Try to stay close. It could be crowded inside."

Rebel resisted a moment, then followed me inside. I wanted to turn around and run. Charlie grabbed my hand as we joined a suffocating swarm of people. We weaved through rank bodies going in all directions at the same time. My neck pulsed, and breathing was hard in the stifling air. I focused ahead, straining to see the heads of my family. The crowd thinned as we neared a back-corner blockhouse. The overwhelming noise from barking dogs, loud music, and jumbled voices still pounded in my head.

"Catch your breaths here," Papa shouted over the noise. "I'll see about accommodations."

I searched my family's faces, making sure no one had gotten lost. All seemed overwhelmed, and speaking was impossible.

Charlie tugged on my hand. I squatted to hear him say, "I need to pee."

"You have to wait until Papa shows us where to go." I stood, scanning the fort.

It had four blockhouses in the corners with family-sized cabins nestled between the tall log walls and back gate that was bolted closed. I shuddered at the greater need for protection. I located a few privies but hoped we would be able to use our own bucket once settled somewhere.

Charlie continued to squirm and grimace.

Papa stepped out and waved for us to follow.

We came to a stop in front of the opposite corner's blockhouse. Charlie let go of my hand and ran to the side of the structure, wiggling his hips. I kept my eye on him while Papa spoke. "Sorry, we have to bed down in this storehouse with another family for the night. Help me unpack the horses."

Charlie returned, grinning and waiting for Papa to give him something to carry inside.

As we unloaded, a throng of people gathered to welcome us. The chaos was too much. I stepped away, removed my bonnet, and used it as a fan. I wiped sweat from my temples and sucked in a deep breath while I observed the activity in the yard.

A group of young children laughed and squealed as they tossed a pig bladder back and forth. Women and older children tended to the late afternoon chores of cooking supper and folding laundry. A waft from crisp sheets flapping in the breeze reminded me of home. I shook my head, amazed that so many families braved the dangers of settling so far west. *Maybe some of these will travel with us tomorrow.* I turned to Rebel, removed his saddle, and then pulled out the curry comb. The neighbors dissipated as I brushed and patted my gelding's neck.

Momma stepped out of the storehouse, caring a ladder-backed chair past me to a large oak tree. My siblings moved as one toward the children in the yard. "Have fun, but watch out for each other." She sat with a sigh. "Land sakes. I've never seen so many helpful people all at once."

Papa stepped around his horse and smiled. "Did you find a place for us inside?"

She nodded. "Yes, and Mrs. Davis helped. She insists on sharing her stew with us for supper and won't let me help. Just wants me to enjoy resting." Momma looked at me. "Go enjoy some time with other girls. Mrs. Davis's daughter is your age. Her name is Eliza."

"Are you sure you don't need me?" Part of me hoped she did as shyness rose.

She grinned and shooed me away. "I'm sure."

Katie and Lizzy were standing among a group of girls as I eased toward them. Everyone stopped talking and looked at me.

"She's our eldest sister, Mary." Lizzy grabbed my sleeve and pulled me closer.

I smiled. "How do you do?"

After they gave me their names, Katie spoke. "They were telling us about the Boone girls. We'll meet them when we get to Fort Boonesborough."

"Oh. Please continue." I hung back a little and allowed Katie to resume her position in the center.

The girl named Eliza eased up to me and whispered. "You missed them raving about Jemima Boone. But these girls were her friends and thought too highly of her. The real Jemima is bossy and mean. I didn't like her much, and she didn't like me. Would you like to take a walk?"

Not sure how to react, I nodded. *At least I can find out what she had against the girl.*

We found an open space near the storehouse and sat on the ground.

"What did Jemima do that turned you against her?" I straightened my petticoat.

She gave me a wide-eyed look. "Do you already know her?"

"No." I shook my head. "I'm just curious. How long did you know her, and what happened?"

Eliza cleared her throat. "We arrived here in April because of the Indian raids. She was the first to introduce herself to me and invited me to have tea with her and the other girls. At first she was nice enough, but a few days later, I noticed her whispering something to one of the girls who had waved to me. They laughed and walked away." Eliza hugged her knees to her chest. "On another day, I approached the girls to visit, and they continued talking to one another, but not to me. I found out later that Jemima told the girls my family was too Injun and not acceptable company." Her eyes watered.

I huffed. "Your skin isn't that dark, but what does that matter?"

She picked up a twig and snapped it. "My momma is a granddaughter of Jacob Cassell's second wife, a Cherokee. But my grandmother and my momma married white. It's not my fault."

"Oh. Cassell's Woods is named for your family?" I sat back, stretching out my legs.

"Yes. My great-grandfather Jacob is German. He came here years ago, acquired this land, and his first wife from the Shawnee. He doesn't live too far away." She sighed. "As more settlers come to the area, his Indian family isn't acceptable. My Cherokee people have moved away, and as soon as my papa and older brothers find us a place in Kentucky, they'll come back for us. We aren't going anywhere near the Boones though. I don't want people knowing about my Indian side. I'm tired of the looks."

"How long has your papa been gone?"

"About four days."

"Well, I lament the fact that we're going to Fort Boonesborough." I placed my hand on her shoulder and looked her in the eye. "If we ever meet again, I promise not to tell anyone."

She smiled and stood with a sniff. "Thank you. I see my momma carrying the stew to the table. I have to go help with the young'uns."

"I'll check in with my momma, too. I'm not in the mood to visit with those girls, anyway." I rose and walked beside her.

Eliza went inside, wiping her eyes with her apron.

Momma glanced up as I approached. "I must have dozed. Did you have a good visit?"

"Yes, ma'am. I like Eliza. Where's Papa?" I scanned for him.

She smiled. "Off somewhere talking with the men, I suppose. After he brought bags of grain and venison jerky, he said something about a map Daniel Boone had left for him."

Mrs. Davis cleared her throat behind me. "Sorry, to interrupt. Supper is ready if you want to gather your family."

"Yes, ma'am." I turned back to the yard and rushed to the girls first. "Time to eat. Find the others while I locate Papa."

One of girls snorted. "You're going to eat with Injuns?"

I whirled back around. "Better than eating with imbeciles." *Did I just say that?* I laughed and headed to the blockhouse where we had stopped upon arrival.

I waved to a man who came out the door. "Excuse me, sir. I'm looking for Michael Shirley. Is he inside?"

"Yes, lass. Need me to fetch 'im?" He grinned.

I shook my head. "Just tell him supper is ready. Thank you." I darted back through the crowd.

Katie stood in my path with hands on her hips and a frown on her face. "Why were you so rude to Anne?"

I stopped and glared. "Did you hear what she said?"

She wobbled her head. "Well. The Davises do have Indian blood, and we are eating with them." She sounded snide.

"How dare you look down on people based on what others have said? Don't become like those snooty girls. They're the ones who are rude." I resisted the desire to shove her as I passed.

A makeshift table near the storehouse was set with steamy bowls. Papa arrived with George shortly after I sat beside Eliza and Momma. The Davises also consisted of a four-year-old girl named Charlotte, and two boys of eight and six named Zim and Ned, whom George enjoyed talking to more than eating.

Other than too much salt for my taste, the venison stew was good and was complemented with hoecakes. Papa sat back and belched. "Good stew, Mrs. Davis. Thank you. I hear there was some kind of commotion here a while back." He grinned.

Mrs. Davis smiled. "Suppose I should tell the women's side of the story you must have heard from the menfolk."

Momma tilted her head.

Papa laughed. "Yes, ma'am. My family enjoys a good story."

All eyes stared at Mrs. Davis and waited. Eliza chuckled.

Mrs. Davis folded her hands in her lap. "At the end of last summer, Captain Boone left with a group of men to clear the brambles from the trail to Kentucky. The remaining men decided to leave the gates open for a breeze while they played ball in the front field and tested the quality of the corn liquor."

Papa laughed, holding his belly. I gazed at him and frowned. *Nothing funny about raids.*

Mrs. Davis smirked. "Well, a group of us women were in a fit about the lax security. We were afraid of renewed Indian raids. So, Mrs. Boone and Mrs. Carr devised a plan to scare the men to their senses. Several of us loaded rifles and sneaked into the woods outside the front gate."

As Mrs. Davis spoke, my heart sped.

She wiped sweat from her forehead and took a breath. "The women inside the fort closed the gates and barred them without the men's notice. In a few minutes, those of us with rifles got off a volley of shots at trees. We heard the men hollerin' and hootin'. We had a great laugh before making our way back."

Momma snickered, then laughed so hard she snorted, which set off the rest of us. Mrs. Davis went on with the story while we composed ourselves.

"When we arrived, the men yelled and cursed. Some wanted us whipped, which set off two or three fistfights. Mrs. Boone calmed the men by threatening a formal charge of dereliction of duty in the protection of the fort residents. They dropped their heads and sauntered away. The men have remained diligent ever since."

"I would hope so." Momma beamed with a chuckle in her voice.

I snickered. "Did the women on the inside let them in?"

"No." She laughed. "When the men couldn't get the gates open, they hoisted a young man up so he could climb over the picketed walls and open the front gate. The men still outside 'bout trampled one another as they ran through the pond to get inside. All the while, the women huddled together in the yard, pretending to be scared."

Papa smiled as he stood and stretched. "It's good to get this side of the story. The men made it out to be the women overreacting with no need to put on so." He laughed again, then scanned us. "It's time my family head to the pallets and try to sleep. We have a far piece to go tomorrow. Say good night." He stepped over to Momma and helped her up.

"I'm looking forward to meeting Mrs. Boone." She grinned at Papa.

He pulled her into his arm and held her. "I thought you might."

I had mixed feelings. Mrs. Boone sounded wise, but her daughter Jemima wasn't going to find favor with me.

Chapter Fourteen

August 31

In the morning, Momma managed to stave off heaving by chewing peppermint leaves while we ate a quick breakfast outside with the Davises. We loaded supplies and said our good-byes. In the hazy light, I scanned the inhabitants of the fort as they tended fire pits, livestock, and other chores. No one else appeared to be leaving.

"Safe travels." Mrs. Davis kissed Momma's cheek and stepped back. "My man was wearing a green linen shirt when he left here with my older two sons. Tell them to come fetch us if your paths cross."

"Why not come with us?" I glanced between Mrs. Davis and Papa.

Papa nodded. "You'd be welcome, and we can get a later start. It looks to be about six miles to Blackmore's Fort."

"I best wait here for word, but thank you for offering." Mrs. Davis smiled.

Eliza waved and returned to brushing her little sister's shiny black hair.

Nancy handed Papa the grapevine. He notched our ninth day and then we headed to the gate. We traveled westerly along the trail, and my thoughts turned to Hans Mueller, Beth Dunkin, and Eliza Davis—three people I'd call friends if we met again someday. I sighed and joined Charlie in singing the frog courting song.

At our first hour break, Momma walked over to Papa. "I need a slower pace, please."

He nodded. "Do you want to ride for a bit?"

"Yes. Maybe that will help." She stepped into his arms. "I'm sorry. I just don't have much strength today."

Morning sickness had weakened Momma more than I'd ever seen and worry crept in. *What can I do to help?* I glanced around at the foliage and trees. "Is there anything growing here I can use to make a remedy for you?"

She turned toward me and shook her head. "I've been watching for dandelion leaves, but I think the season is past. Everything else will be too strong."

"We'll stay at Blackmore's a few days so you can recover," Papa said.

Momma shook her head.

"Don't argue." Papa's tone was firm. "You're too weak to continue."

He wouldn't say that unless he's worried.

At the second hour, Momma dismounted and smiled. "I feel much better. No need to delay travel tomorrow. Since we're getting to the fort by noon, I'll have a good rest and be able to eat better."

Papa raised his eyebrows. She stepped away from him, took Sally's hand, and led her horse to the small creek.

Katie glanced at me as if wanting to ask about Momma. I shrugged and led Rebel to a clump of grass.

Within a mile of Blackmore's Fort, sounds of civilization drowned out the peace of the forest. Once again, pickets loomed ahead. This fort was smaller yet louder, and I didn't see any children about as we entered the gate. A handful of women mingled around a group of men who were touching them in places that made my jaw drop. I averted my eyes and rushed with Charlie to catch up with Katie and Lizzy. *I'm not liking this place.*

"Welcome, folks." A scruffy elderly man greeted us. "We have a cabin, if you care to stay."

Papa shook his hand. "Yes. We would. Thank you."

"Come this way." He escorted us to an available cabin built into the picketed wall.

After we secured the horses and supplies, Papa wiped his brow. "We need shade. Help me make a canopy. We'll attach a rope between the cabin wall and that tree." He pointed.

With our small tent canvas secured overhead, we gathered underneath and took turns dipping water from a bucket into our cups. I poured half a cup down my blouse before sitting on the ground, wishing for a leaf fan. Momma passed out jerky for lunch, but I wasn't too hungry.

In a few minutes, Momma rose and rubbed her belly. "I'm taking Charlie and Sally inside for naps. Looks like the people are getting ready for a celebration of some sort. I hope it won't last all night. Maybe the rest of you can find fresh game and prepare something for our supper. I need to lie down the rest of the day." She took the two youngest children's hands and entered the cabin, leaving the door open.

Papa stood and stretched. "You girls stay here under the canvas. George and I will go see about things." He handed me the extra rifle. "These men look rough. Keep this handy."

"Yes, sir." I gulped.

As they walked toward the blockhouse, I scanned the area. A few men were nearby but ignored us. Most of the inhabitants of the fort were scurrying around the central yard, setting up a platform. In front of that, several men laid planks on the ground like a floor.

"I bet there's going to be a dance tonight. I saw a man carrying a fiddle, and it looks like a dance floor out there," Katie said. "Otherwise, why would they be putting down a floor in the middle of the yard like that?"

I nodded. "But I don't think we'll be attending. Papa said this is a rough place."

"We'll, maybe we can watch until it gets too wild." Lizzy smiled. "We could have our own dance."

"Maybe." I shrugged and glanced at the acorns Susie and Nancy had collected into a pile. Nancy grinned. "The acorns are fairies, and we're going to make them a house so they can have tea."

I chuckled until I looked beyond them. A disheveled man staggered out of the next cabin and spit a long stream of tobacco juice, allowing some to dribble down his chin. He turned toward us, grinned with rotted teeth, then raised his hunting shirt and wagged his genitals.

I gasped, then stood, grabbing Nancy's and Susie's hands while turning them away from the sight. I stepped into Katie's and Lizzy's view. "We have to get inside the cabin—now." I rushed them into the cabin and shut the door.

Momma sat up.

"I'm sorry. We had to come inside." My heart raced. "A man just exposed himself to us."

Momma's nostrils flared, and her eyes narrowed. She rolled off the bed and went to Papa's pack. She removed the hatchet and stepped toward the door. After standing there with her hand on the latch, she took a deep breath and turned back to us. "Don't go outside unarmed." She placed the hatchet on the table and lay back down. "Try to be quiet and let me rest."

"Yes, ma'am," we all whispered as one.

My sisters stared at Momma with frightened faces. I scooted a chair by the window and sat with the rifle in my lap. *Momma with a raised hatchet—another unshakable image.* I sighed. "I'll keep an eye on our horses and supplies."

A few moments later, Papa and George approached; each carried one end of a spit pole with a hunk of meat. They stopped mid-yard and placed the spit across the fire pit's forked sticks. I motioned for my sisters to follow me outside.

Papa frowned as we neared. "Why were you inside?"

Katie gave a quick explanation.

Papa glared toward the vile man's cabin, then turned to George. "Go guard Momma. I'll guard the girls and help with cooking."

Papa turned the handle of the spit for a good thirty minutes, and juices from the venison shoulders dripped onto the oak logs in the fire. The sizzle sent luscious smoke wafting into the air, and my stomach growled.

"These are ready. Let's take them to the table to cool." Papa lifted one end of the pole and I raised the other.

Momma greeted us from under the tent canvas that now sheltered the table. George must have helped her bring it out of the stuffy cabin. We sat on log stools, and

Papa prayed. As we ate, I allowed myself to relax in the hot late-afternoon breeze.

In a little while, fiddle strings whined into a peppy reel I recognized but didn't know the name of. I wanted to dance.

"Let's get inside." Momma stood and rushed the younger children inside. Papa held his rifle barrel over the crook of his arm and stared down a group of drunken men nearby who gawked at us girls. They sneered, then returned to frolicking with the women.

Back inside, Papa lifted a chair and sat it by the window. "We're getting out of here first thing in the morning. We'll take turns keeping a gun aimed out this window toward the horses—one-hour shifts until midnight, then I'll take the rest. George will be first, then Momma, Katie, and Mary. If anyone approaches our horses, shoot."

My gut knotted with the memory of shooting Isaiah Brown in the knee so he couldn't harm me. *Please, God, keep evil men away from our horses and keep us safe.*

"Turn in and try to sleep." Papa readied the rifles, stood one butt-end on the floor, and gave the other to George.

When I opened my eyes and saw Papa still at the window, I hurried to take my turn. "Why didn't Katie wake me?"

"No need," he whispered. "All's been quiet. I took over from Momma. Go ahead and sleep."

"I can't." I carried a chair over to Papa's and stared out the window. "I'll just sit with you then." The full moon cast eerie shadows among the trees. *How can such a beautiful place be so treacherous?*

Gunfire erupted.

Momma sat up. The younger children piled around her. Loud cursing outside was followed by another volley of gunfire.

"Stay on the floor." Papa motioned, then hunched down with his gun pointed near the horses. "Grab a rifle and keep watch. I'll go see what's happening."

"Michael, don't." Momma leapt to her feet and rushed to him.

Papa wrapped his arms around her. "I'll be careful."

She stepped back, and he eased to the door. "I'll knock twice when I return."

I couldn't breathe. The room spun. I flashed backed to that night on Hans Creek when gunfire erupted all around me. *I must get to Rebel and escape.*

Someone sat me in a chair. "Mary, it's Momma. Breathe. You're safe. Look at me."

I sucked in a deep breath and focused on her eyes. I couldn't speak. After two knocks on the door, Papa entered and lighted a lantern. "Men were shot stealing supplies. Let's get loaded and move out. The moon is bright enough to light the trail."

Momma spoke something in his ear. He squatted before me and rubbed my arm. "I'm sorry, polliwog. We're going to be all right, but we must hurry. Take deep breaths."

Breaths remained shallow. I couldn't stand. Momma handed me a blanket. "Fold this. Small tasks help settle your mind."

Papa, George, and Katie went out the door while I tried to fold the blanket.

"Be stwong." Charlie took my hand and tugged. I pushed off the chair and stood on wobbly legs, gulping back the bile in my throat.

I squeezed his hand and breathed deep. "Thank you, little soldier."

He smiled and led me outside to Rebel.

Papa passed us, giving instructions. "Walk beside your horse—keep it in front of your body like a shield."

My mind remained in a stupor as we double-timed some distance away before stopping.

When we came to a small creek, Papa turned to us. "We'll cross in the morning. Find a spot on the ground and try to sleep a little. Loosen the saddle cinch but don't unpack anything."

Sleep? How can I sleep? Every creaking tree branch startled me. Scurrying creatures made my heart race. I rolled onto my back and stared past the tree's silhouetted limbs at the starry sky, guessing the time as one o'clock.

Chapter Fifteen

September 1

A terrible groan startled me. I turned my head in the darkness toward a soft sobbing in the woods and stood. As I eased toward the place, a man's silhouette rose from behind a crop of bushes. I gasped and jumped.

"Stay back, Mary." I sucked in a relieved breath at Papa's firm voice.

"What's wrong?" I whispered.

The next groan lasted longer, and my heart wrenched. *It's Momma!* As I turned away, her sobs followed me. I sat on the ground sniffling and allowed tears to roll down my cheeks. *It's something bad.*

"What's happening?" Katie asked and sat up.

"Momma's sick." I sniffed. "Go back to sleep." I couldn't bear to say more.

A moment later, Papa stepped from behind the bushes. "Take everything across the creek and set up the tents by lantern light. Leave my horse." He took the tinderbox from his saddlebag and handed it to me.

"Is Momma...?" I hushed.

"Momma is losing the baby." His voice was raspy. "Shouldn't take too long. I'll bring her across later. Try not to worry the children. Find a secluded spot for the small tent for Momma and me. Everyone else in the big tent."

I couldn't move. *Momma's never lost a baby before.*

Papa touched my arm. "She'll be sad and drained for a few days, but she should recover. We'll wait until she's ready to move on. Until then, take charge of the camp and the children. Leave Momma's medicine pack on the ground here."

Momma moaned, and Papa rushed back.

I squatted beside Katie, who had remained seated. "I don't know how much you heard, but we have to wake everyone and get across the creek to make camp." I wiped tears. "Just tell the children Momma's sick, and we have to leave her alone. If you didn't hear, I'll tell you later. We have to get going." I scooted to George next. "Wake up. Papa wants us to cross the creek and set up camp."

George jumped up, rubbing his eyes. "Why can't we make camp here?"

"Because Papa said so. Momma's sick. No more questions."

My groggy siblings followed me to the bank. "Mount the horses. They can see in the dark better than we can. I'll take Sally. Charlie will ride with George."

The moon's glow sparkled in the shallow water as we crossed. The trickling current soothed my nerves—but only for a moment. Once on the bank, a burst of energy sent me into a tizzy. When I halted, Rebel snorted. I handed Sally down to Katie and dismounted. "Wait here while I see where to set the tents."

Using the large butcher knife, I chopped through a tangle of vines and found a clearing that would work for Momma. "Set up the small tent here."

I returned to a larger clearing, near the creek, but on a rise. "Big tent there. We'll make our beds in the big tent and let Momma and Papa have the small tent."

"What? I don't want to share a tent with all the babies." George huffed.

"If you want to sleep in the open, go ahead. But Momma needs seclusion while she gets better. Now hush. I have to light the lantern so we can set up the tents. We'll set up the big tent first and get the children settled." I went to find the tinderbox.

George, Katie, Lizzy, and I managed to set up tents in the dim lantern light while Susie and Nancy kept Sally and Charlie awake long enough for us to roll out pallets. I stepped back to Rebel, slipped the hammer into Papa's tool pouch, and looked toward the sky. I couldn't discern the time of night or even find the North Star. Tears flooded my eyes and dribbled down my cheeks. *I need sleep. God help Momma.*

As I returned, George and my sisters stood on the bank peering across the creek.

"What's wrong with Momma?" Lizzy sniffed.

Susie and Nancy rushed to me as I sat on the ground.

Katie stepped closer. "And don't say she's sick again. Something's wrong, and we need to know."

I took a deep breath. "The baby in Momma's belly is being born behind those bushes. But it's too tiny to live. Papa will bury it there and then help Momma across."

"Poor Momma," Susie said.

"That's why she needs her own tent, so she can rest today. When daylight comes, we'll have to work together and try to be quiet. We need to try to sleep now. I can't think anymore."

George stood and pointed. "They're coming."

I rose, shielding my eyes from the moonlight.

Papa's arm was around Momma's waist as they crossed. Little Sis followed without a lead. Drummer leapt across the creek and shook off when he reached us.

I darted to Momma and whispered, "We set the small tent up for you over there." I pointed to the location. "The children are asleep in the big tent."

"Thank you." Her voice was raspy. She sniffed. "I'll undress and hand my clothes out to you. Weigh them down in the creek. Wash them out later." She squeezed my arm. "Don't worry. I just need to rest now." Her hand dropped to her belly, and she moaned. Papa helped her away and inside the tent.

I waited a moment, then eased to the tent and waited. Papa peeked out, handing me the soiled garments. "Tell George to bring a saddle over here. Oh, and bring a clean bucket of water. That's all for now."

"Yes, sir. I'm sorry about the baby." I fought the lump in my throat.

He touched my hand and nodded. "Go now." The flap dropped.

I blinked away tears, rushed to the creek bank with the blood-soaked chemise, and called out, "George. Take a saddle to the small tent and leave it. Someone bring the water bucket. Papa needs fresh water before I rinse this chemise."

Katie filled the bucket and carried it away before I dunked and rolled a large rock on top of the blood-tinged gown. After drying my hands, I crawled into the tent.

Drummer growled at the unmistakable squabble of coyotes on the other side of the creek. I burst into sobs along with those still awake. *God, please spare Momma from hearing those growls.*

As dawn broke, I crept to the small tent and whispered, "Papa." I didn't raise the flap for fear of seeing Momma exposed. There were no sounds of movement. *How am I to wake Papa without waking Momma? I'll just have to speak normal.* "Papa. Should I send George and Katie to hunt for small game?"

Papa peeked out. "No. I'll go with George." He kept his voice soft. "I need to scout the area, anyway."

I nodded and stepped back as he scooted out on his rump, then pulled his boots on. His disheveled hair and the dark stubble on his face made him look scruffy. He stood and stretched.

"Do I need to take care of Momma while you're gone?"

He shook his head. "No. Her bleeding has slowed down like her monthly. Just bring fresh water, and she'll clean up and come out when she's ready. You're in charge of the camp until I get back. Keep the children quiet and don't let them bother her."

"Yes, sir." I sighed.

Papa strolled to the big tent to wake George. I peeked at Momma. The quilt covered her as she reclined against the saddle, asleep. *I'm sorry, Momma.* I let the flap fall. Sadness about the lost baby made my chest hurt and my eyes water.

I lifted the water bucket and walked to the supplies. Katie and Lizzy were there, locating the cooking utensils.

"I need to get Momma's chemise washed. Can one of you please refill her water bucket and leave it by the tent?" I dug into the saddlebag and found the lye soap.

"I'll take it." Lizzy grabbed the bucket and walked with me to the creek, peppering me with questions. "Did you talk to her? Is she getting up?"

"Dip the water and take it to the tent. Then come back here, and I'll tell you. Don't try to talk to Momma. She's still asleep."

Lizzy collected clean water upstream from the chemise and hoisted the bucket to her shoulder to tote it.

I hope most of the blood has washed away. I removed the rock and doused the garment a few times to wash away the pink tinge. Laying the garment on the stone, I wiped it down with soap, and then rubbed the spotted areas together until the cloth was spotless. Pleased with the outcome, I rinsed, wrung out the water, and spread the chemise on a bush to dry in the sunlight.

As I returned, Katie beamed and pointed to the small fire she had started. I nodded. "Good job. Have you figured out what to do about breakfast? Should we just eat jerky again until Papa and George come back?"

She nodded and placed a larger stick on the fire. "How is Momma?"

I waited for Lizzy to step around me and sit on the ground. "Papa said she's going to be all right. We have to keep the children quiet and away from her tent. Momma will come out when she's ready."

"We should do some foraging, I think. If Papa says it's safe." Lizzy glanced around.

Katie nodded and turned to stir the fire. "We should also make stew. We can find roots and add the dried vegetables and jerky. Then if Papa and George return with squirrel or rabbit, we can toss them in."

"I'll make coffee. Papa will enjoy some after being awake most of the night. Let's eat some jerky now; then we can wake the children. I'm starving." I went to the supplies, and Lizzy helped me carry packets, the pot, and dishes.

Katie returned from the creek with water and dumped some in the pot. I positioned the trivet over a pile of stones I had placed in the center for more heat. "We need to keep the fire and smoke low the way we've been doing."

We took turns adding a handful of carrots, peas, and spices to the pot. I allowed Katie to taste and say when it was enough.

Once we sat down, I passed around jerky

"This is a good day for the children to practice reading and spelling." Katie bit off a hunk of jerky.

I nodded. "Good idea. Staying busy is best. Wake the younger children now."

George held up a skinned squirrel as he and Papa entered the camp. "Brained this one with a rock." He brought the squirrel to Katie and whispered, "We couldn't use the rifles. Fresh moccasin tracks."

Blood rushed to my feet. A scream lurched in the darkness of my mind. Katie eased the squirrel into the pot. I caught my breath and shook my head as I reached for a pouch of jerky. "Breakfast time."

Susie peered around Papa. "Is Momma going to eat?"

"No, I'll take her some jerky if she's hungry later." He looked exhausted.

Nancy brought the grapevine to Papa, and he added the tenth notch before putting a small log on the fire. "I'm going to check on Momma." He glanced at each of us as he stood. "Don't worry. She'll feel better in a few days." He rubbed his chin and looked at me. "We're three days from the protection of Martin's Fort. We can return to Blackmore's until she's stronger, if we must."

Leaves shuffled outside the small tent. *Momma.*

"Good afternoon." Momma's voice was hoarse. "Stew smells good."

She was dressed in her spare chemise and petticoat. Her hair hung unbraided and wet down her back. Papa rushed to help her sit on a stump. She held her arms out to Sally. "I can't lift you, but I can hug." The toddler lay her head in Momma's lap.

Charlie stepped up and gave her a hug. "Momma sad?"

She nodded. "Yes, and tired. But in a few days, I'll be all right."

The rest of us stooped to kiss her cheek and then sat on the ground next to her.

I choked back tears. "I'm sorry about the baby."

She stroked my head and nodded. "Thank you for washing my chemise."

"What can I do for you now?"

"Take Sally." She pried the child from her lap. "Sit with Mary. I want to talk to everyone, and then I'll go back to the tent and rest until suppertime."

Sally plopped into my lap.

Momma grimaced, shifted her position on the stump, and took a deep breath. "Losing a baby in the early stage is uncomfortable and sad, but not unbearable. I've released our babe to God. By morning, I will be able to walk slowly and excuse myself to the woods from time to time. But I will recover and be stronger each day."

I stared at Momma and stood. "But Papa said we can go back to Blackmore's, so you can rest. I think we should go back to the Dunkins' place."

"Take a deep breath, Daughter, and calm down. I've already had this conversation with your papa. We're going on to Fort Boonesborough." Momma's brow rose in defiance. She peered at Papa. "I want to continue our journey to Kentucky, and that's final. I don't want to go back, and I don't want to stay here another day and be sad."

I lowered my eyes and shook my head. "Yes, ma'am."

I took several deep breaths with watering eyes. *How does one acquire such strength?*

Papa helped Momma back to the tent. My siblings and I ate jerky and for the first time, I realized I didn't have to be in charge by myself.

Chapter Sixteen

September 4

The rolling terrain gave way to a flat clearing, and we came upon a rippling stream. Papa glanced over his shoulder at Momma. "Will a short break do? We're a few hours from Martin's Fort."

"Yes. I'm doing well." She smiled and found a shady tree to sit under. Sally plopped down beside her and cuddled.

It had been two days since she'd lost the baby, but she had insisted on leaving the place the following morning. We had traveled at a slow and sad pace, but this morning Momma smiled, and a rosy glow had returned to her cheeks.

I led Rebel to some grass and sat with my back against the tree. Papa and George studied the ground as they walked together toward a large birch tree, searched around it, then rushed back with large eyes.

Papa glanced at each of us. "Sorry, we won't be stopping again for a while." His tone made my heart flutter. "Go relieve yourselves now and mount your horses. We have to ride hard."

I took Charlie's hand and led him to the bushes.

He stood with his arms crossed. "No pee."

"Papa said we have to. We won't be able to go later."

He managed a few drops.

"Go stand beside Rebel, and I'll come in a minute." I relieved myself, then dashed over to the tree. Three diagonal white lines were painted on the smooth beige bark with a red slash across them.

I rushed back and grabbed George's arm before he could mount. I leaned to his ear. "Were they...the number of scalps taken?"

He nodded, then frowned. "And recent. The paint is still bright. Papa said a day or two back at the most." I released his arm, and he mounted.

My neck pulsed, and my breaths were shallow as I climbed into the saddle and pulled Charlie up. We trotted behind Lizzy and Susie for almost an hour before we stopped at a creek to let the horses graze and drink.

Papa seemed less stressed, but still serious. "Another hour from here. Pull out some jerky and munch on the way. We need to get to the safety of the stockade."

I sighed. *Papa hasn't smiled in two days. I miss his playfulness.* I grabbed a handful of oak leaves from a sapling and tossed them at him, grinning. "I love you."

Charlie giggled and rushed away to gather leaves.

Papa stepped backward and laughed as he brushed leaves from his hat. "I love you too, little polliwog." He smiled. "Are you getting too old for me to call you that?"

"I'll always be your little polliwog." I stepped into his arms and felt at peace again. "Just don't say it around my friends...whenever I have friends." I stepped back, grinning.

Papa chuckled. "You're growing up too fast and beautiful. I'll have to keep my rifle handy when all the suitors come calling for you at Fort Boonesborough."

"Oh, Papa, stop that." I laughed. "If you scare away all the suitors, I won't have a husband, and you'll never be an *opa.*"

His eyebrows rose, then he grinned. "I aim to scare off all but the suitable ones. Now, let me pay attention to the surroundings again." He kissed my forehead. "I enjoyed our lighthearted moment. I hope life won't be so serious once we're settled again."

About midafternoon, pickets appeared through the trees ahead.

Papa yelled, "Hello at the gate."

"Incoming family," a young man shouted and waved us in.

He tipped his hat at us and smiled. I couldn't help return it. He was handsome and tall and conducted himself in a confident manner.

Martin's Fort was a small stockade with six log cabins, but the security seemed alert. *Impressive.*

We passed a man planing pine furniture. He glanced up with a nod, but continued to work. There were no children or women about that, I could see as we dismounted at the busiest cabin.

"Wait here while I check in and make a report about the painted tree." Papa went inside.

I glanced back at the gate. The man tipped his hat again with a wide grin. I chuckled and turned front-facing, waiting for Papa.

He emerged from the cabin smiling. "Wonderful news. There is a new cabin available for us to bed down in tonight. The owner said he would bunk with friends. He said I could help him plane boards for a new table in thirty minutes as a barter. After we get settled, I'll take George with me."

Momma nodded and hugged Papa. "I'm so happy I could cry. I'm not going to be in a hurry in the morning. I want to enjoy resting in a safe place."

Me too. Tears of joy filled my eyes.

Papa nodded. "Agreed. We need rest, and this place seems peaceful. Everyone head to that middle cabin." He pointed. "After we unload, someone can go to the spring outside the gate for water."

"I'll go." Katie grinned and glanced toward the gate.

I elbowed her. "Pshaw, not by yourself."

"Girls." Momma's tone was firm, as if she'd already perceived our mischief.

How is she so quick? I shook my head and smiled.

After we unpacked, George and Lizzy had charge of grooming the horses. Katie and I helped the younger children make pallets along three walls of the small cabin's dirt floor. With the final pallet made along the back wall, I rose to ask Momma about going to the spring. She and Papa were in the front corner alone.

Momma snuggled her head against Papa's chest in a long embrace. He whispered in her ear, then kissed her neck. They lingered there as if oblivious to everyone in the room. I couldn't look away. There was something sacred in the moment. My eyes watered.

Katie bumped my arm and tilted her head toward the door with the water bucket in hand. We motioned the younger children outside.

George glanced at the door. "Papa coming?"

"In a while. He's busy." I grinned and stepped away with Katie. "We're going for water."

I scanned the gate area as we walked, then frowned at Katie. The young man was no longer there. In his place was an elderly man who grinned while ogling our chests.

When he didn't acknowledge our faces, I stormed in front of him.

His head jerked up as he stumbled backward against the wall, bounced back, and then stared at my eyes.

My heart raced as I stood and glared. The curses I wanted to spew hung in the back of my throat.

He shook his head and stepped back, blinking. "Why you bewitchin' me that a-way?"

Katie pulled my arm and stepped in front. "We're going to the spring to fetch water for our family."

"Spring's near that big oak." He pointed while glancing at me and then at Katie. "Is that girl daft?"

"Sometimes." She sighed and pushed me toward the spring. "What's wrong with you? Why were you so rude?"

My head pounded. I stood still and sucked in a deep breath. "He was staring at our chests. He's the rude one."

"Ew, I didn't notice." She laughed. "I reckon he was a might disappointed by our lack of breasts."

I huffed. "We need to stay together and not let our younger sisters go off alone. Papa's warned us about the lax morals in some people."

I plucked a couple of pine needles from a sapling and chewed on one to ease my headache.

As we returned through the gate, I stopped in front of the man.

He flinched. "What is it, girl?"

I narrowed my eyes. "You're a—"

Katie grabbed my arm. "Stop this—or I'll tell Papa."

I stepped away with Katie, took a deep breath, and then blew it out.

"What were you going to say to him?" Katie turned to me with a frown.

"Never mind." I shook my head. "It's too shocking to say aloud."

She grinned. "It's good you didn't say it, then. The man would have told Papa, and you'd be in trouble."

"True. But I should have at least called him an old fool." I bit down on the pine needle and entered the cabin with Katie.

Papa and George came in for supper scented like pine. Papa laid a slab of smoked venison on the table and began carving it. My eyes teared from joy.

George beamed. "Mr. Sweeney said Papa, and I did good work. He went to the smokehouse and came back with this meat. Said he figured we were tired of jerky."

"God bless Mr. Sweeny." Momma unpacked the plates.

After supper, I carried the bucket of used dishwater and a soft horse brush to our picket line a few yards from the cabin. Rebel nickered. I stepped over and rubbed his neck. "Ready for a washing?" I wet him down and chatted. "I miss doing normal things like this. Maybe once we're settled again, we can go on a quiet picnic and relax under the shade of a big oak tree." He shook off water and bumped my arm. "Oh, you want more attention?" I rubbed him down again, then tossed the water toward the fence. When I turned around, the young man from the gate strolled toward me, smiling, and tipping his hat.

My breath caught.

He stopped in front of me, laughing. "Mr. McKeeney left guard duty a couple of hours ago, pointing you out. He said, 'That fiery-eyed-serpent-girl is daft. I reckon she would'a gouged out my eyes if her sister didn't pull her away.' But you don't seem like a lunatic, and I like fiery women. You'd make a fine wife. I'm James Thomas Appleton. J.T. for short." He grinned.

I sighed and peered into the sky. *God, why are there men like this?* "Well, Mr. Appleton, any man who thinks a fiery-eyed-little-serpent-girl would make a fine wife is a dad-blame fool. Leave me alone, or I'll yell for my papa to teach you proper manners."

He looked past me and took a step back, clearing his throat. "No need, miss." He tipped his hat and headed to one of the cabins near the blockhouse.

Someone snickered behind me. I turned my head and jumped at the sight of Papa. My cheeks grew hot.

"Good job, polliwog." He laughed. "But someday a man will ask to court you, and he won't mind a little fire and venom from time to time. You're a lot like your momma." His eyes sparkled.

My jaw dropped. "I'm like Momma?"

He nodded. "Except for the cursing part. You've picked that up on your own."

"Sorry." I looked at my feet.

"I've said worse. Just don't let Momma hear it. She'll give you that look she has." He chuckled.

I nodded. "She'll make me swallow straight vinegar. I called Katie a mean name when we were little. I know not to say anything bad around her."

Papa lighted his pipe and smiled. "Want a puff? It'll help you calm down."

"No, sir." I laughed, remembering the time he let me try it a few years ago. "Don't like the taste so much. I like the scent of beechnut in the smoke though. I need to go to rinse the bucket in the spring."

"Go ahead. I'll watch out for you from here." He puffed out smoke, and I breathed in a whiff before heading to the gate.

As I squatted at the spring and dipped the bucket, three men gathered at a nearby oak tree. They didn't seem to notice me as they passed around a pouch of tobacco.

"We gotta join the Continentals. Thar ain't enough men ta beat the British." The younger of the men spoke with an impatient tone.

"And if we don't win?" An older man stood with folded arms.

The first man spit. "We hang as traitors."

"The dang Shawnee are countin' on us joinin' so they can wreak havoc on the settlements and force us out." The older man's tone grew more serious. "Draggin' Canoe is stirrin' up his Chickamauga band of Cherokee to raid in the spring."

My heart raced. *George said something about a man dragging a canoe. Maybe it's this Cherokee.*

The third man shook his head. "Yeah—that Henderson's a fool encitin' folks to their death out thar in Kentucky. I ain't gonna waste my life protectin' settlements from Injuns when I can give my life for the winnin' of 'em. And if'n we win the war, we come back an' claim what's ours—make 'em pay for allying ag'in' us."

No militia protection at Fort Boonesborough? Ringing in my ears gave way to pressure in my head.

The young man spoke again. "I've been ta the place. They done built cabins too near the Cain-tukee River bottom and in-betwix two high ridges. All the Injuns have to do is stand up thar and pick 'em off. Ain't no 'mount o' cheap land worth losin' wives and babes for."

I stood lightheaded, and my gut wrenched. I wanted to run, but my feet wouldn't move. *We can't go. I must get to Papa and tell him these things.*

"I'm with John." The third man nodded. "Joinin' the Continentals is a worthier cause. I'm gonna head east in a day or two. Get outta here 'fore winter."

I forced a step and stopped, trying to suck in deep breaths, but it was too late. Bile rose in my throat, and I dropped to my knees, heaving.

Papa squatted beside me. "What's wrong?"

Uncontrollable trembling made my teeth chatter. I couldn't speak or move.

Papa lifted me in his arms and carried me to the cabin like a baby. He bumped the door with his foot, and someone opened it. He set me in a chair, and I bowed my head, covering my face with my hands. Momma placed a wet cloth on my neck.

I raised my head. "We...can't go...to Kentucky." I swallowed. "Those men said—"

"Sh. We'll talk about it later." Papa bent to my ear. "You're in shock. Rest now."

All I could do was stagger to my pallet and lie down, weeping and shaking. I was so frightened I couldn't sleep. I remembered Papa saying Fort Boonesborough was six days away. *What then? Are we fleeing yellow jackets to land in a hornet nest?*

Chapter Seventeen

September 5

My mind was as hazy as the morning. I watched myself roll pallets, fold blankets, and gather outside with my family for breakfast. Conversations took place around me, but nothing made sense. I sat down beside Drummer, stroking his head, and smiled when he rolled to his back for a belly rub.

Papa squatted in front of me and raised my chin, peering at my eyes. "I want you to ride today and follow behind me. Charlie will walk with George until you feel better." He pulled me to my feet and into his arms. "Don't lose hope."

I kept my voice low. "But...there won't be militia protection at Fort Boonesborough. Those men said Cherokee will raid this spring."

"There may be Indian raids, but I'm part of the militia, as are the other men. Colonel Henderson is negotiating for Virginia troops. Trust in divine protection and lay down your fear. Focus on helping Momma and your sisters. I'll cut the fourteenth notch on Nancy's vine, and we'll go." He kissed my forehead and turned to the waiting family. "We'll cross the Cumberland Mountains and make camp in Kentucky tonight."

Cheers erupted from everyone but me. I wiped tears from my cheeks and went to Rebel, hugged his neck, and breathed in his musky scent. "You'll take care of me, won't you, boy? You got me away from those Tories; you can get me away from Indians." I reached into my pack and pulled out my neckerchief, allowing the items wrapped inside to fall out among my garments. There was something comforting about draping it over my shoulders, if just for a moment. I had dreamed of wearing it at my first dance. *Not likely now.* I folded it neatly and laid back in the pack, then lifted my petticoat and mounted.

"Look. A rainbow." Nancy pointed to the western sky.

Momma shielded her eyes. "It is wonderful."

"Maybe it's a good sign." Lizzy smiled at me.

I squinted at the streaming beams of light. *There it is.* I'd never seen a full arch stretch across the sky. *God's promise to himself not to destroy us by flood. Maybe it is a good sign. Please, God, I need it to be.*

Papa shook his head. "Rainbow in the morning could be a warning. Most likely we'll meet a storm somewhere by this afternoon."

Wonderful. I sighed, then felt pangs of guilt. *Sorry, God. I'm thankful we haven't been through storms thus far.* I mounted Rebel and urged him into a smooth gait behind Papa, ignoring J. T. Appleton's wave.

As we entered the dark, shadowy forest, my stomach fluttered. I wanted to flee back to Indian Creek at a fast gallop. *I'd rather hang as a traitor than face capture by Indians.*

Papa reached for Rebel's rope and grinned at me. "I'll lead you for a bit."

How did he know I was about to bolt?

Papa let me walk again when our trail became steep and rocky. We passed gray boulders covered in patches of bright-green and pale-gray moss. At one place, the trees were so large the sunlight couldn't break through. It reminded me of the dark creek bottom where the black bear chased Rebel away on my journey home to Indian Creek. I sucked in a deep breath to slow my racing heart. *Why can't I calm down?*

Rebel's head bobbed, as if keeping time with the frog courting song Charlie hummed, and then a turkey gobbled from the northern ridge. My body stiffened, and I stood still. *Indians?* I held my breath. Papa looked back at us with his finger to his lips and stood still.

Drummer stood erect, sniffing the air. His body remained west-facing, but his ears rotated north and south.

Papa turned his head to the right and then to the left. He nodded and waved us forward. I breathed shallow, willing each foot to raise and lower in light steps as I listened to the forest. *How can he tell it's a turkey gobble and not an Indian?*

Small springs trickled from crags in the boulders and made the trail damp in places. A lush assortment of ferns benefited from the constant wetness. Patches of wild strawberries were left void of red berries as we passed.

Papa stopped in a small clearing and pointed to the tallest mulberry tree I'd ever seen. "Stand back." He walked down an incline to the trunk and shook.

A hail of elongated berries bounced on the ground. "Eat only the firm black ones."

We converged, eating the sweet, juicy berries as fast as we could. Their tiny seeds were almost undetectable. I paused between bites. "These are the best I've ever eaten."

"A nice blessing." Momma stood with a handful. "Mulberries have a short season."

Papa wiped his lips. "That should sustain us up to the top. Let's go. We're about to be in Kentucky." His smile and gleaming eyes reminded me of an excited Charlie. I laughed and collected a few more wonderful morsels into my mouth before taking Rebel's rope.

The fast-paced hike along the shaded path soon brought us to a narrow clearing between the cliff walls. Drummer peered into the sky with his ears pulled back and whimpered. I squinted at the clear view of the afternoon sky awash with glinted thunderheads sailing east. I went to him and knelt to scratch his ears. "Sorry, boy. Maybe it will keep moving away from us."

"Leave the horses and follow me up this ledge." Papa hacked briers away with his hatchet.

When I reached the ledge and stood, my breath caught—not from the view of the valley below, but because it was of Kentucky. A shiver ran down my back. My childhood lay behind me, and an uncertain future lay beyond the steep green mountains and across the valley below.

I lifted my petticoat toward Kentucky in hopes of a refreshing breeze until I spotted four men ascending the trail where we left the horses. Papa walked down to meet with them. I snatched Charlie as he peered over the ledge. "Stay back; you'll fall." The rush of fear made my head pound.

George eased his rifle from General and watched Papa, but the men chatted in a lighthearted manner, and Papa waved to them as they tipped their hats toward us and continued along the trail headed southeast.

Papa returned, smiling. "Scouts headed back to Moore's Fort. They said the trail to Fort Boonesborough is clear and friendly. Said the Shawnee are staying north, preparing for winter."

My shoulders relaxed. For the first time since we left Indian Creek, worry over being attacked by Indians left me with a deep, relieved breath.

"Can we talk again?" Lizzy asked Papa.

"I think it'll be fine for today. I'll quiet you as needed. We're still six days from the fort and need to remain watchful. Let's get on down to Kentucky. We have a creek to cross before making camp tonight."

My chemise was damp from sweat beneath my bodice. I flapped the cloth with my hand and blew air in a futile attempt to dry my chest, then stood, shaking my petticoat loose from my legs before walking.

Papa meandered down the mountain trail at a diagonal to prevent the horses from sliding on the loose rocks. But the horses remain surefooted as we made the trek.

"Are we in Kentucky now?" Nancy asked.

Papa beamed. "Yes. On the count of three, everyone shout 'huzzah' one time. One, two, three."

I shouted as loud as I could. Our voices seemed to swirl and hang in the air above our heads with the blackening clouds. "How much further to the creek?"

"I'm guessing within a half hour or so, but we're stopping as soon as I spy a suitable place to shelter. Those thunderheads aren't moving away; no time to dally." Papa quickened the pace.

The frightening blackish-green sky crackled and boomed as we gathered under a grove of wind-whipped sycamore trees. Drummer cowered and peered up, trembling.

Papa motioned us to the center. "Pile your bedrolls here so the younger children can sit on them while we hobble the horses. I'll picket them high between these young trees, and then we'll drape the large canopy over the picket line. We'll hunker down on the bedrolls awhile. Seems to be moving fast."

Momma and Lizzy removed bedrolls, then handed them down to Susie and Nancy, who ran them to the place Papa selected. Charlie and Sally pounced on top as if it were a fun game. The horses accepted the hobbles without balking. Papa and I secured the picket rope high enough above the horses' heads so that the draped canopy wouldn't annoy them.

With a clap of thunder, the wind blew small limbs from treetops. Nancy screamed. Sally whimpered, and Charlie dove deeper into the bedding. The horses jerked their heads.

Papa and George pulled the large tent canvas from Gideon. "Get under the canvas, and hold it up while I tie it off."

The younger children sat huddled together. The rest of us held the canvas as Papa tied it sloping downward, and then we ducked inside. Drummer snuggled as far into my lap as he could. Acorn-sized hailstones pelted the canvas from time to time and bounced on the ground around us. Wind gusts whipped through the canvas, misting us with rain. The horses bobbed their heads, and Gideon shifted his hooves a little.

"Stay on the bedding, and don't touch the ground," Papa shouted over the noise.

Lightning flashed with a terrible explosion nearby. I screamed, clenched my teeth, and gripped my bedroll tighter. "At least we're not in a cave down in a gully." My face grew hot. I never told them about my blunder the night I delivered the dispatches. When our cave flooded, Rebel and I had been forced to rush to higher ground.

Papa chuckled. "I would hope not. Never shelter in a gully. Sounds like the hail has ended."

After what seemed like half an hour, the thunder ended and light rain trickled through the leaves. Papa glanced out. "We can move the horses out now, but we'll stay camped here and let everything dry out."

Rebel whinnied as I untied his rope and spoke in soothing tones. "There now. It's over." I rubbed his neck until he calmed.

Momma stood and stretched. "Time to find out how good our waterproofing has been. We'll be sleeping a bit soggy all night, though."

After piling the supplies under the tent, we brushed the horses and Gideon and let them graze. When we crowded back inside, I wiped my face and chuckled at my waterlogged family, shaking my head. "So much for this morning's rainbow being a good sign."

"Well, we didn't drown in a flood, now, did we?" Papa laughed.

"No, sir." I half-smiled.

Momma passed around the jerky. "I'm thankful we're in one piece. And look—our waterproofed bags have saved our provisions." She held up a packet of carrots we had dried in the sun back in May. They were still shriveled.

As a light rain drummed on the canvas, I stretched my legs across the wet grass and bit off some jerky. The sweltering heat and body odors in our crowded tent were inescapable, and we'd be soggy all night. I scooted closer to the slight breeze.

"We'll wait in camp until noon tomorrow to allow everything to dry. Shouldn't take long in this heat." Papa wiped his brow.

Momma nodded and fanned her face with a corner of her apron. "And if the creek's not too flooded when we reach it, we'll take lye soap to ourselves." We laughed and nodded.

Papa stood. "The rain's stopped. George and I'll go see how far the creek is from here and bring back water and small game for supper, if we can." He looked over at me. "Scrape tinder from some saplings, and we'll scout out some dry wood for a fire."

"Yes, sir."

I took Papa's ax to a nearby tree and whacked off the outer bark of a young oak, then scraped the dry middle into my apron. Momma and Katie dug a shallow pit, and the others filled it with small twigs and acorns. When my apron was full, I squatted in front of the fire pit and tucked my shaving in among the kindling.

A twig snapped in the woods, and my breath caught. Papa and George stepped into the camp carrying tree shards. "Lightning provided a nice cache of dry timber for our fire." Papa smiled over his armful. "The creek isn't far, but we didn't collect water. Didn't want to get stuck in the mud and lose our boots. Maybe it won't be too marshy tomorrow. Least it's not too deep to cross." He and George placed their piles on the ground, and Papa arranged a few shards in with the shavings, then removed the tinderbox from his pouch.

"No game around yet, either." George stood, shaking his head as he let the water-bucket handle slide from his arm.

Momma handed him a rope. "We'll make do and be grateful. Come help me hang a line for drying out our bedding when we wake in the morning."

We sat around the smoky fire eating from our stores, then Momma pulled the vicar book from a waterproofed bag. "It's a good time to read."

I was happy the vicar's prison term for debt was overturned in chapter twenty-eight. But upon learning of Olivia's death, Sophia being kidnapped, and his son imprisoned for taking revenge, I wanted to throw the book into the fire.

Momma stretched out on her soggy bedroll. "Time to bed down and try to sleep."

I closed the book with a sigh. "May we please read on until something good happens? There're only four chapters left."

"No. It's too dark to see now, and I don't want to waste our candles." Momma held out her hand, and I gave her the book. *It better end happy.*

Papa nodded. "We need our rest. Once we cross the creek tomorrow, we'll have the Cumberland River to ford. If it's flooded, we'll have to swim."

As my youngest siblings lay on their pallets, my breaths shallowed with the image of Charlie being swept down

Indian Creek back in May. *How do we swim across a swift, flooded river with babies?*

Chapter Eighteen

September 6

George and Papa rushed into camp from the wooded area northeast of the trail. They had gone to find the reason for a horrible stench that blew in with the midmorning breeze after breakfast.

"We have to go now." Papa's voice sounded tense. "No time to explain."

George was solemn and pale. I followed him to the makeshift clothesline. "What was it?"

He jerked his blanket off the rope and stood blinking his glistening eyes. "Dead men."

I gasped and stepped back, clasping my chest.

He sighed and folded his blanket in half, then again before rolling it and peering at me. "Papa thinks they were Mrs. Davis's husband and two sons. One of them wore a green linen shirt like she described."

Tears welled in my eyes.

He stared down at his boot. "They were too—" He looked at me. "Well, remember the figures painted on that birch tree two days back—before we arrived at Martin's Fort?"

All I could do was breathe.

He turned away, wiping his cheek on the sleeve of his shirt. "Papa reckons they'd been there near a week and the scouts didn't smell anything. The rain freshening them again's the reason we caught wind of them. There's not enough left to bury. Papa said we need to get away from this area in a hurry. When we get to Fort Boonesborough, Papa will make a report." His gaze dropped as he shook his head. "Worse than seeing those men hanging back at Elk Garden."

I rushed from him and allowed tears to fall as I finished securing saddlebags to Rebel. I knew from George's reference to the painted tree that the men had been scalped. Soon there would be no evidence of them or even a marked grave. Mrs. Davis wouldn't receive the news from a courier for a week or more. I didn't know how to pray for them. *Strength? Comfort?* None of these seemed appropriate. I wanted to go to them—put my arms around Eliza and cry with her.

Papa mounted. "Let's go." His urgent tone sent a shiver up my back.

I dried my face and hoisted Charlie into the saddle, then climbed behind him and urged Rebel into a trot.

Papa kept us at a gallop for about a mile before stopping in front of a thick canebrake. "We'll have to dismount and walk through this mess to cross the creek ahead. Give your horses a lot of slack. Stop and shout if you see a snake."

Sharp green blades scratched my arms while I defended my face from the slaps of tall stalks of cane swinging back from George's assault through them. Charlie kept one arm up while he held onto my petticoat.

When the ground became marshy at the creek, I released Rebel's rope. "You'll have to follow me on your own now." I lifted Charlie into my arms and scanned ahead for dangling snakes or slithers through the muddy water. He clasped his arms around my neck as I navigated the shallow rocky creek. On the other side, briers hung from the cane Papa had hacked with his hatchet. "You have to walk now." I lowered Charlie to the ground.

An hour later, the trail became a pleasant forest floor again, with occasional rocky and spring-soaked areas, but the sound of rushing water made my blood run cold. My family gathered at the bank of an enormous fast-flowing river. *How are we going to cross this?*

"Unpack the horses while George and I make a small raft for the supplies," Papa shouted above the roar.

My stomach knotted.

Momma gazed at Papa. "Land sakes."

He took hold of her hand. "Don't worry. I'll stretch the ropes across for a ferry line we can hold on to."

Papa removed the ax from Gideon and went into the woods with George, who carried the rifle. The rest of us unloaded the horses. In a few minutes, chopping ended with Papa yelling, "Timber" to the cracking sounds of a mid-sized post oak tree crashing to the ground. Chopping resumed until George and Papa walked back leading Gideon, who was dragging four cut logs tied together with braided vines.

We piled everything in the center of the raft and waited. Drummer rushed aboard and plopped on top of one of the packs, wagging his tail.

Papa tied one of the long ropes to a sturdy tree and carried the other end with him to Little Sis. He gathered her lead and that of Gideon, General, and Sir, and then stepped into the water. "I'll take them across. George will follow me with the raft." He laughed at our dog. "And Drummer."

He held up the other end of the rope. "After unloading the supplies, I'll secure the rope and ferry the raft back for Momma and the babies." He looked at Katie and Lizzy. "Your horses will swim with you on top, so stay calm and hold on. I'll watch from the bank in case you need help." He looked at me. "You'll cut the rope loose from the tree and tie it around Susie's waist before mounting."

I took a deep breath and gazed at Katie, Lizzy, and Susie, who were staring at me.

George waded with the raft into the flow of the river. I held my breath as he rippled diagonally in the current behind Papa and sighed when they reached the bank on the other side. He and Papa unloaded the raft, and then George stood guard while Papa secured the rope to a tree and gave it a good jerk. Papa boarded the raft and shoved away from the bank, holding on to the rope as he pulled himself back, grinning. "As you can see, our little ferry works well."

Momma nodded but frowned and glanced back at me and my sisters. "I can't believe you're having the girls come over alone. Please bring the raft back for them."

Papa smiled. "They can do it, Katherine. I won't have strength enough to come back again. Have confidence in your horses, girls, and hang on."

Momma took the youngest children's hands, and after stepping onto the wobbly logs, she sat in the middle. Sally and Charlie plopped into her lap, and Nancy huddled beside her, hanging on to her arm. When Papa shoved off the bank, I turned to my sisters. "You can do it."

Katie nodded and rode Rusty into the river. Lizzy took a deep breath, mounted, and then rubbed Patriot's neck before easing him forward.

Land sakes. I can't watch. But I couldn't look away. I waited until they were safe on the other side before I sawed the rope end loose and quickly tied it around Susie.

After we mounted Rebel, I took a deep breath. "Good boy. Let's go for a little swim."

Rebel waded into the current and stood still a moment. I didn't rush him. He bobbed his head once, and I stroked him. "It's all right." He stepped along the riverbed, and when he became buoyant, my heart raced.

Susie held on to his halter. I squeezed his body tighter with my thighs.

"Oh no," Susie shouted.

Before I could grab her arm, she fell into the river and sank. I screamed, "Susie," and scanned the water, hoping to see the rope and pull her back. But she was gone. She popped up a few feet away, sputtering and gasping as she thrashed the water in a panic.

"Turn over and float," I yelled, then screamed toward Papa, "Susie fell in." *God, save Susie.*

She rolled over and allowed the current to carry her downstream, where I lost sight of her again. Tears streamed down my cheeks, and my heart raced. Papa was already on Little Sis, riding into the river and hoisting the rope as fast as he could. Rebel found his footing, and I rode him up the bank, praying and peering at Papa. Momma and my sisters were crying and watching the river. George stood down the bank.

When Susie appeared limp on the other end of the rope, I held my breath and wiped tears from my eyes. *Is she—?* Papa lifted her onto his mare. Susie coughed and cried in his arms. I burst into tears and dismounted. George rushed back toward us, shouting. "Susie bumped her forehead on a rock, but she seems all right."

I wiped away tears and rushed into Momma's arms. "I don't know what happened. She was holding on and then—" I couldn't say anymore.

Momma sniffled, squeezed me, and then stepped back with a turn and ran to Papa's horse.

"Thankful for swim lessons." Papa handed a dripping-wet Susie down to Momma and dismounted with a sigh. He stood there shaking his head, out of breath.

I put my arms around Susie's drenched body. "I'm sorry I couldn't catch you. What happened?"

"My hand cramped." She sniffled. "I let go to re-grip but couldn't."

Momma felt of the red welt on Susie's forehead and then looked into her eyes. "Are you hurt anywhere else?"

"No, ma'am—just exhausted." Susie sighed and put her arms around Momma's neck, weeping. "I was so scared."

Papa stroked Momma's back. "After I recover my senses, we'll get a few miles away from this river and make camp." Papa knelt and spoke to Susie. "You can ride Momma's horse."

She nodded. Momma snuggled Susie to her chest a moment longer, still sniffling.

Papa lay on his back. "As long as the weather holds, the remaining river crossings will be easy, and we'll be at Fort Boonesborough by week's end."

I took a deep breath and sat beside him. Tears filled my eyes again. "I'm sorry, Papa. It all happened so fast, and she was gone."

Papa sat up and wrapped an arm around me. "Not your fault. You're the one who reminded her to calm down and float. All is well." He sighed. "Five more days, and we'll be at the fort."

I rested my head on his shoulder. "Why can't we make camp here?"

"Too many trails converge at this river. I'd rather be more secluded."

I bit my lip. *More secluded? From what?* I decided not to ask.

Chapter Nineteen

September 11

Peace came each evening Papa, George, and Drummer returned from scouting an area without seeing Indian signs. On our fourth night away from the Cumberland River, we took turns reading the last chapter of the *Vicar of Wakefield*. In its surprise ending, Olivia was found alive, but her marriage to the vile Squire Thornhill was deemed legal, which restored her reputation but bound her to the scoundrel for the rest of her life. *I suppose the moral of her tale was the reason for Momma's 'guard your heart' caution back at the Muellers.* I chuckled at the memory.

Nancy handed Papa the grapevine this morning, and he added the twentieth notch. "Time to get going. We'll be in our new home by tomorrow afternoon."

Sweet words to my ears. The forest scenery had become mundane and mind-numbing.

When we came to another canebrake, I lifted the hem of my petticoat and weaved through a tangle of vines. I sighed at how frayed it had become. *How long before we have cloth enough to make new clothes?* I smiled. *At least I have an outfit to wear for a harvest dance...*I gasped as something sharp stabbed into the arch of my left foot.

Raising my leg revealed a piece of cane protruding from the worn-out sole of my moccasin. I clenched my jaw and wiggled it free. The shard had a diagonal cut as if hacked low to the ground by a previous traveler. Blood dripped from my foot. *I need to stop the bleeding in a hurry.* I tossed the stob away and remembered that the bandages from the Muellers were still in my apron. I stuffed one through the worn raw hide sole and into the stab wound, gritted my teeth, and continued the hike. *Now what? This is going to become inflamed.*

About midmorning, we came out of the cane near the bank of a small creek. "We'll graze the horses and rest a minute," Papa said.

When no one was watching, I pulled up a cluster of plantain leaves and sat on the ground, then removed my shoe and the blood-soaked cloth. This time I packed leaves into the wound, wrapped my last bandage around it, and slipped the moccasin back on. *Sure wish I had some of Mrs. Mueller's salve. It worked wonders on my previous wound.*

A twig snapped, and Drummer growled at the woods to my right. I glanced up as six shrieking men with red chests leapt from the bushes.

I clasped my throat, unable to scream. Drummer lunged into the air and caught the arm of the man rushing toward me with a raised tomahawk. The man howled and plunged his knife into Drummer's chest.

"No," I screamed as my beloved pet yelped and fell to the ground. I scrambled to my feet, picking up a large rock. The brave held his bleeding arm and glared at me with large dark eyes. A tuft of black hair sat atop his red-painted head like a bird plume. I glared at him, ready to crack his head open if he neared. *Get up, Drummer!*

Another brave stepped in front of me, yelling unintelligible instructions as he pointed toward Momma, who was behind me. My sisters and the younger children were huddled with her, sobbing. I gritted my teeth from the pain in my foot and rushed to Momma's side, scanning for George and Papa.

Next to the horses, a brave held a knife at George's throat, but my brother didn't squirm. Two other braves held onto our horses and Gideon. Blood trickled down George's face from a cut above his eye. *God, please don't let them take George away.*

No. I gasped at the sight of Papa lying on his back behind the horses. He was pinned under the foot of a brave, who was clad only in red leggings and a blue breechcloth. Papa yelled as the brave grabbed a handful of Papa's hair and jerked his head back, raising a large knife.

I stepped forward in a rage. Momma clutched my arm and stared into my eyes. "Be still." Her tone was firm as her eyes watered.

Papa threw the man off and stood, but the brave lunged and slashed Papa's right thigh. He fell, and the brave rushed toward him again with the bloodied knife.

Suddenly, an older brave yelled and rushed toward him. The younger brave snarled like an angry dog, spit in Papa's face, and kicked him in the ribs.

One of the braves with George shouted something to the others and ogled me, Katie, and Lizzy. His red-stained face had a black line painted across his forehead, with streaks down his eyelids and nose. He jumped in front of me.

I stepped back, unable to breathe, but glared at him with all the venom I could muster—daring him to touch one of us. *I still have my rock.* He moved closer, and I gripped my weapon tighter.

The elder brave shouted and waved him away from us. After growling, the younger man worked his mouth as if collecting spit. I did the same. He spewed in my face—I doused his. He stormed away, and the others laughed. I dried my face with my apron.

They released George, and he ran into Momma's arms, crying.

My gut wretched as the six braves mounted our horses and led Gideon away with all of our possessions, including our rifles. *Leave food and water.* Heaving breaths accompanied bawling as Rebel disappeared into the forest. *My Rebel.* Bile rose.

My sisters and brothers sat together in a heap on the ground, sobbing. I hobbled to the bushes and threw up. Still trembling, I crawled to the motionless body of Drummer and placed my hands on him, hoping to feel life. Weeping, I scooped his limp body to my chest, refusing to say the words.

"He's dead." Momma said it. "Lay him under the bush and gather fresh oak and plantain leaves to help stop Papa's bleeding. We must hurry." She sounded scared.

Her words jolted me. *Papa could die?* My stomach knotted.

"Wait. Come." Papa motioned with his head as his hands held pressure on his bleeding leg.

I hugged Drummer for the last time, laid him on the ground, and willed myself not to look back as I limped to my family. Papa bowed his head. "Thank you, God, for sparing our lives." His voice quavered. "Please help us make it to the fort." He sniffled and scanned our faces. "I'm sorry I didn't listen to the warnings." He drew a deep breath and sounded exhausted. "We shouldn't have traveled alone like this."

"Papa, don't die." Lizzy dropped to her knees and hugged his neck.

Momma pulled her back. "Hush that kind of talk. You're scaring the younger children. Get the leaves."

Tears wet my checks as I stooped toward Papa and kissed his sweaty forehead. "Be strong." I gulped back tears and hobbled to the creek bank with Katie and Lizzy. We didn't talk. My mind numbed as I plucked leaves. Everything replayed, and I cried for Drummer. *My little hero.* I sniffled and picked a clump of sage leaves.

Katie held up a piece of birch bark with curved sides, like a bowl. She whispered, "We can use this for water." She stared at the creek. I'll go dip some for Momma." She untied her apron with one hand. "Can you come get this?" her voice quavered.

I limped to her and caught the apron and its contents with mine. My heart raced as she took a deep breath and ran to the creek, scooped water, and rushed toward Momma without spilling too much.

Lizzy showed me the comfrey leaves she'd found but didn't talk. Her eyes flitted from me to the woods as we walked back and emptied our aprons beside Momma.

"Good job, girls." She glanced up from holding pressure on Papa's thigh. Her eyes were red and swollen. "Please see about the younger children; they're too quiet and still. Console them."

My legs wobbled as I sat on the ground and waved for Charlie to come to me. Tears welled in my eyes as he plopped into my lap and cuddled to my chest, still trembling. I held him and sniffled. *We could all be dead now—or captives. Death would be better.* George sat down beside me, holding his legs to his chest, and rocked. Katie and Lizzy huddled and cried with Susie, Nancy, and Sally.

Momma grimaced as she removed the blood-soaked cloth from Papa's thigh, and my stomach churned. *That looks bad.* I couldn't suppress the gut-wrenching sobs any longer as I rocked with Charlie.

When I looked at Momma, she was packing a handful of crushed leaves into Papa's wound.

"Whoa-ow. That hurts," Papa yelped.

"The sage oil will keep this from festering, I hope. Only God knows what was on that filthy knife they stabbed you with. Now, get ready. I'm going to poke some more."

Papa placed his hands on the ground and closed his eyes.

"Poor Papa." Katie winced as she cuddled Sally.

I held my breath as more oak and plantain leaves were crushed and pressed onto Papa's thigh. Momma glanced at me and then at Katie.

"Oak and plantain leaves stop bleeding. Use sticky comfrey leaves as a bandage only after a wound is clean. I'm using it to secure the poultice."

Her words jumbled in my head. All I wanted to do was curl up in the shade, sleep, and pretend nothing had happened. *I want to wake from this bad dream. Papa's life's not in danger. Drummer is only asleep.*

Momma cut strips of cloth from her skirt with Papa's pocketknife. "Now we need to make camp and forage."

"No. There's no time to lose." Papa took a deep breath and rolled to his good leg and onto his elbow.

"George, go find a straight branch with a fork that I can use as a crutch. We'll go as far as we can before making camp."

"But wha...what about Indians? They're still out there." George stood and stared into the woods.

Papa shook his head. "No. They're in a hurry to get back to their Cherokee village with our horses and supplies. Our bravery and the hand of God kept us alive. Now, we must get to the fort." He frowned. "I'm sorry we have to leave Drummer unburied." Papa grimaced when he stood and limped a few feet away, cursing himself for not traveling with a group.

I rose and looked into the sky, blinking away fresh tears as my sisters and Charlie renewed theirs. Slipping away from them, I plucked more sage and poked it into my wound. It burned like fire, but soon numbed enough to make walking tolerable. I went to Drummer's limp body, knelt, and stroked his fur. My head felt strange—disconnected, as if I was floating. *There wasn't even a turkey gobble to warn us.* "How do I walk away and leave you here?"

Chapter Twenty

The midafternoon heat sapped my energy, and no one had spoken for hours. Charlie hadn't even hummed a tune. My feet moved me along the trail, but each step sent pain up my leg. When everyone stopped to peer at the wide body of water before us, I wanted to scream.

"Is this a creek or a river?" George fanned himself with his hat. "It looks deep."

"I think this is the south fork of Station Camp Creek, a branch of the Kentucky River." Papa's voice sounded raspy. "Daniel Boone called it a creek on the map. Sure wish I'd kept it in my pocket instead of my saddlebag. But if we stay with its northeasterly course, we should come to a smaller creek called Otter sometime tomorrow. One more day from there."

I shook my head. "What difference does it make? How are we going to get across without horses or ropes?" *I can't take anymore.*

Papa glanced at me with drooping eyes and a furrowed brow.

I didn't flinch.

He nodded. "Come, children."

Everyone gathered to Papa with sad faces. Mine tensed.

"It's normal to be angry, sad, or afraid." He shifted his weight to the crutch he held under his left arm. The crutch wobbled.

Is he growing weaker?

He continued. "Every soldier experiences this after a battle. We have suffered wounds, inside and out, and have lost our animals, supplies, and our beloved Drummer." He gasped for a breath.

He is weaker. We need to stop. I glanced at Momma, but she kept her eyes focused on Papa as he spoke. "Now, we must get across this river, and when we're ready, we'll continue to the next task." He held pressure on his thigh and cringed. "Throughout the days ahead, we'll accomplish little things that will rebuild our hope. We'll give thanks to God for allowing us to wake up each morning, and we'll be strong and brave." His face paled.

My eyes watered as guilt convicted me. *Who am I to complain? My family needs me.*

"Now then, find two more logs this size." With another deep breath, he pointed to an arm-sized log. "We'll lie across them and kick. I'll share this one with Momma,

Charlie, and Sally. Katie, Susie, and Lizzy on one log and Nancy, George, and Mary on another."

"I'm ready." Momma stepped into the water, laying Sally across the log on her tummy, and waited as Papa positioned Charlie.

How is she so strong?

Together, they lay forward and kicked across the creek. Katie and her crew set off next. George lay beside Nancy and gave me a salute. "Shove off, matey."

I half-smiled, but didn't feel lighthearted.

When we reached the grassy bank, Papa plopped down and stretched out on his back, gasping.

I stepped on a brier and crumpled to the ground, crying and wanting to scream curses. I took a deep breath. "Can we please make camp?"

"We have to keep going." Papa's whisper sounded raspy.

I gazed at him with my eyes watering. *He's dying.*

Momma grabbed his hand. "I need to check your wound before we continue."

He eased his leg over and straightened it, wincing. The bandages oozed yellowish-green as she removed the bandages from his thigh. "It's festering." Her tone sounded panicked. "We're not going another step until I tend to this. Girls, bring leaves." She squeezed out pus, and Papa flinched.

"I saw a willow tree not too far back." George pointed.

"Go." Momma nodded.

I gritted my teeth and limped to the creek bank, gathering plantain as fast as I could while Katie and Lizzy collected oak leaves. We hurried back.

Momma tended to Papa's thigh, and he yelled the same as when the Indian first stabbed him.

I broke out in a sweat with my heart racing. *God, please. We need Papa. Don't take him.*

Nancy rushed to me with her fingers in her mouth, trembling and sobbing. I squatted down and held her. Urine soaked her petticoat.

She put her arms around me. "Is Papa dying?"

"No. Momma is tending his wound is all." *Please, let him live.*

She sniffled. "I'm scared."

"Me too." I squeezed her hand and glanced at Katie. "Nancy and I will be back in a minute." I walked Nancy into the creek to rinse her skirt and took the opportunity to relieve my own bladder. *God, I read somewhere you wouldn't give us more than we can bear. Is that a lie?*

When we returned, Momma had re-wrapped his thigh with comfrey and the last of the cloth strips. Papa wiped sweat from his brow. Nancy rushed to him, still sniffling, and kissed his check. "Feel better soon, Papa."

"I will, baby. I promise. Go play while I rest." His breaths were shallow as he lay on the ground.

Nancy went to Charlie and Sally, who were sitting with the others near a tree. They all seemed weak. Tears fell down my cheeks at the sight.

George returned with willow bark shavings. "I found a sharp rock to scrape with." He beamed as he laid them on a stump and took a few to Papa.

"Thank you, Son. These will help with the pain and keep me going." Papa half-smiled and placed some in his mouth.

No one saw me stuff plantain leaves and a few of the shavings into my apron pocket. I chewed on a couple and avoided moving.

Momma stood, gazing at Papa with serious eyes. "We're making camp here, and that's final."

I sighed in relief. *Finally. We can tend to ourselves and be strong again tomorrow. Otherwise, how are we going to make it another day and a half?*

Papa stood with his crutch and handed me the tinderbox he carried in his shirt pocket. "Start the fire." He went to sit against a tree.

Momma took Katie and Lizzy to forge for edible plants.

It took my trembling hands longer than normal to make sparks and ignite the tinder. I added small sticks, a few at a time, until the fire was established. Susie, Nancy, and Charlie helped George pile kindling beside me. I added a large log to the fire, then addressed George. "Keep the fire going. I'll help find food."

"Papa told me to whittle a couple of spears for hunting and fishing." He looked up from sharpening the end of one of the straight sticks he'd found.

Papa cleared his throat. "I'll watch the fire and the children. Go forage."

I made my way to a large oak tree and crawled about collecting acorns while a squirrel chattered nearby. "I have greater need of these than you." I threw one at the creature, and it scurried up a tree. "See, you're able to get to another tree. I'm letting my foot rest."

"Are you talking to me?" George frowned as he passed me with his spear in hand.

I shook my head and continued working.

In a few minutes, my apron was full. I returned as Momma and my sisters came behind me.

"We found hickory nuts and mulberries." Lizzy beamed.

Charlie greeted us with a handful of grubs. We all groaned. He pooched out his lips and carried his contribution to Papa.

Papa nodded. "Good job, Charlie."

I dumped my acorns in a pile on the ground. "I've had some before. They're not too bad if you wash them before swallowing and don't chew."

George arrived a half-hour later, toting fish on a vine and a turtle on his spear. We all rushed to him, cheering. Papa smiled. "What a wonderful feast God has provided.

It's been a while since I've eaten turtle, but it tastes like venison."

Momma dug a hole in the coals with a stick, placed the turtle on its back inside, and covered it. "When the shell pops open, we can pick out the meat."

"Turtles have meat?" Susie wrinkled her face. "I thought the shell was its body."

When Momma laid the fish on a hot stone, they sizzled and smoked. After a minute, she turned them over to cook a little longer before removing them to cool. Next, she stirred the acorns and hickory nuts around in the coals. "We'll have to wash off the ashes, but these will be tasty."

"Everyone swallow a grub before Charlie accidentally squashes them." Papa nodded, and Charlie handed each of us one.

Momma passed out the fish as soon as we gulped down the grub. "Be careful of the bones. Not much meat, but better than the grub." She half-smiled.

We were still licking our fingers from the fish when the turtle shell split open with a popping sound. Momma rolled it out of the coals with a large stick and let it cool. She pried the tummy shell from the back shell with the pocketknife and a rock and then removed its innards. "Discard the yellow fat before you eat the meat." She gave it to Lizzy to pass around.

The meat was messy and didn't taste anything like venison, but no one complained out loud.

The small portions of everything we had found were enough to calm my stomach.

"This empty turtle shell, along with Katie's bowl, are fine blessings." Momma held them up and smiled.

Blessings? Only Momma can come up with blessings on the worst day of our lives.

After eating, Papa talked George through making a crude squirrel trap out of sticks and vines. "Set this a few feet from camp, and maybe we'll capture something edible by morning. Go catch more fish. We'll smoke them tonight and add them to our breakfast. Sorry I can't help." Papa looked around at each of us girls and Momma. "There's just enough light left to gather leaves for bedding."

Katie took the other spear and went with George to place the trap outside of our encampment before they headed to the creek.

Lizzy collected leaves with the younger children and piled them where Momma pointed.

Papa spread out on the ground, trembling. Momma poured water from the turtle shell on his neck and wiped his forehead.

"You have fever." Her jaw clenched, and her breaths shallowed.

I can't watch him die. I limped to the water's edge, crying. After removing my moccasin, I plunged my throbbing foot in the cool water.

A twig snapped behind me, followed by a huff from Lizzy. "What are you doing just sitting here?"

I sniffled. "Soaking my sore foot."

Lizzy stepped beside me. "Well, my feet hurt too, but we need to help the younger children gather leaves for our bedding."

I sighed and pulled my foot from the water. "I stepped on a sharp cane stob yesterday. Please don't tell Momma. I'll tend to it and come help."

Lizzy stooped and examined my foot. She gasped. "It's infected. You need to tell Momma."

I shook my head. "She needs to focus on Papa and not worry about me." I stuffed plantain into my wound, then slipped my swollen foot back into my moccasin, gritting my teeth. I stood and then hobbled behind Lizzy to a wooded area. She frowned at me but didn't say anything. I wanted to lie down and sleep where I stood, but instead headed back to the grove of trees, where everyone piled the leaves for our bedding.

Katie and George returned with several fish strung on a vine.

Momma smiled. "How wonderful."

After cooking and cooling them, she threaded a fresh vine through their heads and hung them on a high branch away from night creatures. *Night creatures. And we have no tents for protection.*

"Try to sleep now." Papa spoke in a whisper.

I gulped. Tears wet my cheeks. *What if he doesn't wake in the morning? Stop that kind of thinking.* I smoothed the leaves with my hand and lay down. I dozed until snores and unbearable pain woke me. I rolled onto my knees and crawled to a tree, where I pulled myself up. I limped to Papa's crutch and borrowed it, along with one of the spears for protection, then hobbled to the creek. I sat on the bank and plunged my foot into the water.

The moonlight flickering on the water nauseated me. I lay back on the damp ground, wiped tears away from my ears, and watched a star fall from the sky. Images of Drummer took me back to my ninth birthday when Papa brought me a puppy. I loved the sweet scent of his fur as I snuggled him. I could almost hear his tail thumping the board floor like a drum. His enthusiastic flips in the air always cheered me when I had a bad day. *Who will cheer me now?* Fresh tears forced me to my side. *He can't be gone.*

Papa moaned in his sleep. A shiver ran up my back. *Papa can't go any further.* "Why God? We've made it all this way just to die within a day of Fort Boonesborough? How can you be so cruel?" *If I had Rebel, I could travel in the dark and get close enough to Fort Boonesborough to shout for help. Scouts should be fifteen miles out. But I don't have Rebel.* I seethed. *Damnable Indians.*

I stared into the dark forest, being lured. I shook my head. *It's the fever. I'll die if I try to find my way in the dark.* Shadowy images of bears and men seemed to appear in front of me. I wanted to flee. A crushing pain in my chest made breathing hard. My neck pulsed.

The voice in my head sounded real. *"You and Papa will die here if you don't try to make it to Otter Creek."*

I swallowed the lump in my throat, treated my wound with wilted sage and plantain, and then shoved my feet into my shoes. I stood with Papa's crutch and picked up the spear. My leg lifted in a step, but not toward my sleeping family. I glanced back at them and whispered, "If I can get closer to the fort tonight, I'll have a better chance of being spotted by scouts in the morning, and they'll come for you." *Please, God. Let my body be found by scouts and not by braves...or a bear.*

I focused on the moonlit trail ahead. *If this is the creek Papa thinks it is, it should remain to my left.*

My steps were slow and determined for several minutes. I stopped to verify the northerly direction of the trail and the creek's location.

I couldn't tell which way the trail went anymore, but I followed the creek. I limped and teared up. *I must hurry.* My foot went numb, and my body shivered. My foot felt as if it would explode if I didn't get my shoe off. I plopped back down and attempted to remove the shoe. The sole stuck a little. *No. Not again. This is worse than before. I have to find something to scrape out the infection in the morning.*

A woman's loud scream in the distance sent me crouching on the ground with the spear in front of me, staring into blackness with ringing ears. My heart pounded. *A banshee?* With another scream, I dropped the spear, held my ears, and squeezed my eyes shut. *What is it?* I couldn't move or breathe.

"Get up. Do you hear me?" The voice sounded like Katie's.

I looked up, dazed and nauseated, glancing around for her. No one was there. Papa's words came to me. "We have to keep going—even when afraid." Then it came to me. *That was a panther's squalling.*

My foot was on fire. I tried but failed to stand. *Crawl.* Leaving the crutch and the spear behind, I moved one knee forward. I moved my petticoat and chemise away from the other knee, then moved it forward. *Keep going...Don't stop.* In a few minutes, my knees were raw. I felt my forehead with the back of my hand. *Fever.*

A trickling sound grew louder as I came to a slight decline and damp ground. A few more scoots landed my arms in cool water. *A creek.* I dipped water into my hand and drank. After cooling my face, I managed to sit and soak my foot. I felt around at the plant leaves, plucking some that smelled like plantain when crushed. I rubbed them on my knees, then felt for a sharp rock and hacked strips of cloth from my petticoat. Once my knees were wrapped, I continued down the trail in a painful crawl. The cloth didn't hold, but I cringed and kept going.

I lay on my belly and soldier-crawled with my arms until I collapsed. *I can't.*

My eyes watered. *I'm sorry, Papa.* I rolled to my side and curled into a ball.

Chapter Twenty-One

September 12

The frantic chattering of a squirrel startled me awake in the predawn light. The leaves shuffled, and the squirrel fell silent. I rolled to my sore knees and looked for my spear, then remembered leaving it so I could crawl. I grabbed a large rock and sat dazed—waiting for whatever got the squirrel to come after me.

Laughter? Men's voices? I used a boulder to pull to my feet and peer into the golden hue. The image of a man on a horse. *Are you real?* I waved and shouted, "Help."

As I took a step, the trees danced beside me. Heat burned through the top of my head and down to my feet. *Please see me.*

"I'll take her," a deep voice said. "Hang on, girl."

I couldn't answer or open my eyes.

Along with the sensation of floating in the air, came bouncing.

Shouldn't flying to heaven be smooth? Why am I bouncing?

I forced my eyes open. I was in the arms of a man I didn't recognize. "Are you taking me to heaven?" I whispered.

He smiled but didn't answer. His grip tightened, and we sped through the woods. I couldn't figure out what was going on, but I felt safe and allowed my eyes to close.

Momma called to me from a faraway place as my ears rang. The next moment, George shook me saying, "*Oui-shi-cat-to-oui*, Mary. Be strong."

When my eyes opened again, there was dim candlelight and the scent of stew with hoecakes. My stomach growled. I didn't recognize the small cabin or the young woman with beautiful dark-brown eyes that matched her almost black hair. She might have been in her twenties, but her skin was weathered and tan.

"There, there, be still." She sounded Irish. "I'll be fetchin' your ma." The woman rushed away. A small boy, about Charlie's age, grinned up at me with curious blue eyes and wild red hair. I was weak and groggy, but smiled at him.

Momma entered, crying, and wrapped me in her arms. "You've pulled through." She sniffled and rocked me a minute before stepping back to feel my forehead. "And your fever is down."

I swallowed the lump in my throat. "Papa?" My voice quavered.

"Resting comfortably with another kind neighbor." Momma stroked my head. "You both have serious infections, but will recover in a few days. He'll be relieved to know you're recovering as well. Mrs. Gatliff, here, is a fine healer. We'll have our own cabin in a day or two and be back together. You gave us such a fright this morning when you were nowhere to be found. George noticed the crutch and spear missing. Then we knew you had gone on without us. I'd tan your hide now if I wasn't so grateful you made it far enough to be found. You and Papa wouldn't have made it." She wiped tears from her cheeks.

I sighed. "I don't remember much, but did George tell me to be strong?"

"He did. We all came here to see you when we arrived. He'll be happy to know you heard him." Momma tucked the covers around my shoulders. "Scouts found us midmorning. They said their partner found you at dawn and headed to the fort. They set out to search for others." She kissed my cheek.

"I remember a man's face. Who was he?"

"Sam Henderson." Mrs. Gatliff stepped closer. She wore a simple beige jacket with the sleeves rolled. "Brother of Colonel Richard Henderson himself."

I glanced at Momma. "May I sit up?"

She hesitated a moment, then lifted me while Mrs. Gatliff tucked a straw pillow behind my back. I caught a waft of sage on her hands before she moved back. Moving made my foot throb inside a wad of bandaging, but nothing like before.

The woman peered down at me. "I've set broth to cooling on the table if you wish nourishment."

"Yes, please...ma'am." I smiled.

"No, and it's not ma'am. I'm Christina Gatliff, but you'll call me Letitia if you please. Can I get something for you, Mrs. Shirley?"

"No but thank you." Momma smoothed my hair back and kissed my forehead. "You're well cared for here. I need to get back to the others. I'll come again in the morning. Papa can't walk yet."

I reached for her, and she pulled me to her chest in a hug.

"Good night." My eyes watered. "Hug everyone for me."

She nodded and sniffled, then took the woman's hand. "Thank you again, Letitia."

I wiped tears on my bare arm as she walked out.

Letitia ladled broth into a tin cup and wrapped a towel around it before placing it in my hands. She stayed close as I lifted the cup with both hands and sipped the warm, salty, flavorful broth. "Mmm." I smiled.

She stepped back to the hearth, shifting her pale-green petticoat out of the way as she squatted to tend to her cooking.

"This?" The little boy grinned and handed me a small wooden soldier.

I took it and smiled. "I like your soldier."

"Reese, let her be. Time for bed." She ushered him toward his bed in the corner. "Da will kiss you when he comes in."

I maneuvered my legs to the side of the bed to stand and held the soldier out to Mrs. Gatliff.

"May I help you with dishes?"

Letitia laughed, took the toy, and placed her hands on her hips. "You've just come back from the brink of death, girl. What kind of neighbor would I be, allowin' you to collapse on my floor?"

I smiled, amused at Letitia's wit and the rise and fall of her accent.

"Aye, and now you be snickerin' at me?" We grinned at each other. Letitia continued. "Pleased to have you in my home, Miss Shirley."

"Please, call me Mary."

"Mary, it is, then." She turned to the creaking door as it opened.

A tall, lanky man entered, then hung his rifle on the rack above the door and his hat on a peg before turning. He was the undisputed progenitor of Reese's red hair and blue eyes. "Glad to see you've pulled through—daughter of Cage."

My breath caught.

He stepped closer. "Proud to meet you more proper."

I scanned his face. "How do you know me?"

He grinned. "We met back near Fort Cook with my scouting mate, Reese. Only, we thought you were a dang Tory spy. We took your horse to the fort, and that's when we found out Cage sent you. Now I know why you were such a scrawny lad." He took my hand in his rough tanned one and patted. "I'm Charles Gatliff."

I stared at him a moment as my heart raced, remembering the horror of being left stranded without Rebel. Not wanting to be rude, I replied, "Pleased to meet you." *Why must I keep encountering men I'm trying to forget?*

He nodded and sat at the table.

Letitia returned and removed a cast-iron skillet from the ashes in her hearth. She dumped a fluffy yellow cake onto a clean board and cut it into wedges. Then she sliced a wedge open and drizzled something light brown and thick over it before placing it on the table. She lifted one to a small plate and handed it to me. "Take your time eating to see how your tummy acts."

I took a bite and savored the milled corn cake sweetened with wild honey. I smiled at Letitia. "This is delicious." I took another bite, then made myself stop and sip more broth before handing the dishes to her. "I need to lie back down. My head is spinning."

Letitia placed the cup and plate on the table, then helped me lie down and pulled the covers over me. "No need to rush your recovery. You're not in our way." She felt my head, then wet a rag in a bowl of water, and laid it on my forehead. "I'll be changin' your bandages in the mornin'. Your infection was deep, and I had to do some diggin' and stitchin'. It'll take some time to heal. How's the pain? I can make you some willow tea."

"No. My foot is numb. I'm just sleepy." *And overwhelmed. How did my family survive the trip here at all—and live through that Indian raid?*

Letitia glanced back and smiled. I felt a bond of friendship with her. *Someone I can talk to.* Maybe life here won't be as bad as the men at Martin's Fort predicted.

Thank you, God, for sparing our lives and bringing us here, where we're not alone anymore. I'll find Sam Henderson, as soon as I'm able, and thank him in person. Wait...did I ask if he was taking me to heaven? I hope that was a dream.

I smiled and snuggled under the quilt, at peace with the Lord.

Acknowledgments

Thank you to my family for encouraging me to continue this journey and for understanding my dream.

Thank you to my critique buddies who aren't afraid to challenge my rough drafts.

Continued thanks to C. S. Lakin for professional critiques, edits and guidance since 2008!

Special thanks to descendants of the Duncan family who gave me feedback and final approval for my mention of their ancestors.

I will always be thankful for the family historians who kept the records and stories passed down long enough to be available online for research. Thank you to Uncle Larry who gave me the box of Uncle James' documents to sort out. What an amazing story we almost lost forever.

Special Thanks to Certified Genealogist Patrick G. Megurie for confirming the McGuire sibling connection.

About the Author

 Phyllis A. Still is living her dream as an award-winning author in Texas. She is an eighth-generation descendant of DAR Patriot, Mary Shirley McGuire, the inspiration behind the *Dangerous Loyalties* series. Phyllis loves her family, pets, road trips, history, and playing games with her grandchildren. Her adventurous childhood through seven states created her vivid imagination and a love for stories about people who have overcome hardships.

I love hearing from my readers. Please consider leaving a review online at Barnes & Noble, Amazon, Goodreads, or your favorite book source. Join my Dangerous Loyalties Series fan group on Facebook. Learn more about me at phyllisastill.com

Ready to learn what happens next?

Warrior on the Western Waters

Dangerous Loyalties, Book Three

2022 Literary Titan Five Star Award Winner *Warrior on the Western Waters* is…an emotional roller-coaster of a story and the author effortlessly captures the intense emotions that each character is feeling, which reminds me of the emotional rumination of Suzanne Collins's *The Hunger Games*. Still's writing has a simple eloquence to it. It has a way of leading you through a story with simple language, which leaves your mind free to imagine the intriguing world that she is creating in her book.
—Literary Titan

I review very few American writers, but this is a particularly good historical fiction series that all can enjoy…*Warrior on the Western Waters* is a Miramichi Reader "Pick"! **—Miramichi Reader**

Warrior on the Western Waters, Book Three in the Dangerous Loyalties Series. Inspired by Daughters of the American Revolution Patriot Mary Shirley McGuire.

Far Western Territories, 1775-1776: Lack of security around the Boonesborough settlement allows a traitorous spy to whisk Mary Shirley from her family and deep into Ohio territory. She struggles with fear, prays for rescue, and faces her greatest challenge—survival among the Piqua Shawnee.

For eight months, she learns their language and customs. She cares for her adopted family but longs for her own. A sudden betrayal forces her desperate escape down the turbulent Western Waters toward those she loves.

www.ingramcontent.com/pod-product-compliance
Lightning Source LLC
Chambersburg PA
CBHW070455200726

48293CB00007B/2216